"I didn't give you permission to undress."

Damn him. Not even undressing was to be her choice. Fallon should have been annoyed. But his taking all control had her so aroused that she could barely stand. "May I undress?"

"Are you certain you want to stand in front of me naked?"

"Yes."

"For as long as I like?"

"Yes."

Her nipples tightened and poked into the lace of the gown, showing Kane exactly how much she liked his suggestion. Doing what he wished excited her in a way she hadn't known was possible.

"Fine. Then you may take off your dress. But I want you to understand that you have no rights except those that I give you. You will have no pleasure except what I allow you to have."

Oh...God. She was shaking with the need—he knew exactly how to turn her on, yet he hadn't so much as touched her. And she was going to be standing there naked. Waiting for him.

And loving every second of it...

Blaze™

Dear Reader,

When my Harlequin editor told me that *Beyond the Edge* was going to be the first Extreme Blaze book, my first reaction was *wow!*——quickly followed by the question "How far can I go?"

When she responded, "As far as you need to," I knew I was going to love this project. After all, those are the words that every writer longs to hear. And I had no intention of disappointing.

So I kicked my very vivid imagination into overdrive and wrote an outrageous tale of conflict, love and happily ever after with a good bit of submission/domination thrown in——just for fun.

I'd love to know what you think of this story. You can contact me through my Web site at www.susankearney.com.

Best,

Susan Kearney

Books by Susan Kearney

HARLEQUIN BLAZE

Don't miss any of our special offers. Write to us at the following address for information on our newest releases.

Harlequin Reader Service
U.S.: 3010 Walden Ave., P.O. Box 1325, Buffalo, NY 14269
Canadian: P.O. Box 609, Fort Erie, Ont. L2A 5X3

SUSAN KEARNEY
Beyond the Edge

HARLEQUIN®

TORONTO • NEW YORK • LONDON
AMSTERDAM • PARIS • SYDNEY • HAMBURG
STOCKHOLM • ATHENS • TOKYO • MILAN • MADRID
PRAGUE • WARSAW • BUDAPEST • AUCKLAND

To Brenda Chin, for letting me try
something *really* different.

ISBN 0-373-79222-0

BEYOND THE EDGE

CLASSIFIED
For Your Information.

Read and Destroy.

The Shey Group is a private paramilitary organization headed by Logan Kincaid whose
purpose is to take on high-risk, high-stakes missions in accord with U.S. government policy. All
members are former CIA, FBI or military with
top-level clearances and specialized skills.
Members maintain close ties to the intelligence
community and conduct high-level behind-the-
scenes operations for the government as well as
for private individuals and corporations.

The U.S. government will deny any connection
with this group.

Employ at your own risk.

1

"I'D GIVE ANYTHING to meet a real man." Fallon Hanover sighed into the speakerphone. Easing back in her chair, she ignored the stack of papers on her desk awaiting her signature as well as her view of the twinkling Sunshine Skyway bridge that connected Florida's beaches with the mainland.

Her best friend since boarding school, Jaycee Ketner spoke slowly in her warm Alabama drawl, her voice reverberating through the empty office as if she were there instead of a state and a half away. "Darling, you're just too picky."

Fallon didn't bother keeping her voice down. No one else worked this late. Her employees had gone home to their families long ago, but she'd stayed in a futile attempt to clear her desk. "The last time I wasn't picky, it ended up costing me five million— and that was despite a prenup."

The two women had always been night owls and Jaycee's late-night calls boosted Fallon's spirits. Jaycee might speak slowly, but there was nothing slow about her mind. "Maybe you should give away all your wealth, have plastic surgery to make you ugly and change your name."

Jaycee's sarcasm had pegged Fallon's problem right on the nose. And she appreciated her friend, who understood that there was more to life than appearances and money. In fact, the most important thing—love—had been missing from Fallon's life for so long that she wondered if it simply wasn't her destiny to find that perfect soul mate—a man who loved her for herself.

Perhaps that's why she'd secretly gone to work for the CIA right out of college. The sense of adventure had called to her on a primal level. She'd reveled in the excitement of her secret identity as she'd ferreted out secrets for her government.

Fallon arched her back and rubbed her neck, realizing she'd been sitting so long she was stiff. "What's wrong with a guy wanting me for me?"

"Absolutely nothing. But how can you ever know if a man's attracted to you for the right reasons when you come with so much baggage?"

"Yeah, and I sure messed that one up with Allen." Her marriage to him had been a disaster. The only good thing about it was that she'd refused to allow the experience to keep her from going after what she really desired. Allen had been smooth, sophisticated and wealthy—not as wealthy as her, but comfortable. Once she'd figured out he'd married her only to fund his Internet start-up, she'd cut off the funds and he'd turned nasty. The divorce had taught her to be more careful, but she wasn't so burned that she still didn't believe that the perfect man was out there—she simply had to find him.

"Allen's ancient history," Jaycee said, "but the baggage is still there. Your charity foundation that requires constant direction, a playboy father who drinks from midafternoon until he falls down stinking drunk in the early hours of the morning, a neurotic mother in therapy and on happy pills, and a spendthrift stepbrother who also likes to drink, not to mention that you're the brains behind the Hanover conglomerate's success. What real man wouldn't feel threatened?"

"Jaycee, you aren't helping. I can't just ignore my responsibilities."

"You already know what I think."

Fallon rubbed her brow. "How can I simplify my life? Just suppose I upped and ran away, my father might drink himself to death."

"He's a grown man. You aren't his keeper."

"But it would be irresponsible of me to allow—"

"It's irresponsible of your family to burden you to the point that you don't have a life."

"Sometimes I wish I *could* run away to a place where I had no responsibilities, but that's a fantasy. Too many people depend upon me."

"Did you ever consider that if you weren't there to prop them all up, they'd have to stand on their own two feet?"

Fallon shuddered. "Last time I refused to take one of Mom's middle-of-the-night phone calls, she almost overdosed. I can't have her death on my conscience."

"God…I'm so sorry. Why didn't you tell me?"

"You were on vacation and in love with that Swiss ski instructor. I didn't want to intrude on your fun time." Although her family's wealth meant that Jaycee lived very comfortably, she'd started a magazine and worked damn hard to keep it running. When she'd taken her first vacation in a year, Fallon hadn't wanted to intrude. Besides, Jaycee couldn't have done anything. Fallon had handled it just fine by arranging for the best care for her mother that money could buy.

"That was a wonderful fling." Jaycee's tone softened at the memory. "That's what you need."

"A fling?" Fallon smiled. "I'm not so picky that I wasn't just thinking the same thing. Hot sex. No responsibilities. No strings. You know if I can't have love, I'm just about desperate enough for affection to go for a man who wants nothing more than my body."

"That's the spirit."

"Except as soon as the paparazzi spotted me, we'd be on the cover of every rag. Mom would relapse. My sister would tell me that her kids were taking heat in school. My stepbrother would use my fling to try and undermine me with the stockholders."

"You know what you need?"

"What?"

"A secret identity."

For a second the words hung in the air over the phone line as Fallon's fingers tightened around the receiver. Fallon tried to assess her friend's tone, searched for humor, accusation, *something* to indicate whether Jaycee understood the significance of that statement. A secret identity? She already had one.

Jaycee couldn't possibly know. No one knew that the CIA had, in fact, recruited Fallon right out of college. One of the reasons she'd joined the CIA, other than to help her country, was that she enjoyed adding a little spice to her life while ditching her normal responsibilities. She liked each day to be different—not same old, same old. So while she'd supposedly been touring Europe as a graduation present like most young women in her privileged class, she'd secretly been training at Langley. And she'd proven her worth by partying with a Saudi family on the southern coast of France and successfully picking up gossip that had helped the CIA track Saudi money to terrorist organizations. Fallon didn't believe Jaycee had ever suspected her undercover role, but perhaps she'd slipped up.

"Come on, I have enough trouble being me." Fallon forced a lightness into her tone that she didn't feel. "I couldn't be someone else, too."

"You can do anything you put your mind to," Jaycee countered. "And that includes finding a good man. Your problem is that you're so damn busy solving everyone else's problems that you have no time for your own."

"Nag. Nag. Nag." Fallon teased, though Jaycee's words had struck a chord. Fallon was all too aware of her need to fix the world—ever since she was a kid and her six-year-old friend from across the street had died of cancer. She'd felt so helpless and scared as she'd watched her friend sicken. The adults wouldn't tell Fallon what was going on. As an adult, she'd thrown herself into causes, trying to right the wrongs of the world. Coincidence? She didn't think so.

Jaycee laughed. "I may be nagging, but I speak the truth." She paused. "You need a man to sweep you away from your normal life."

"I think you've been spending too much time editing the fiction stories in your—" Fallon sniffed.

"What's wrong?"

"I smell roasting almonds. Let me call you back." Fallon hung up the phone. Still sitting behind her desk, she tilted her head and inhaled the unusual odor. The last of her employees had left well before seven, and except for the security guard downstairs, she remained the sole occupant of the Hanover Research Institute.

She inhaled again. Could a fire cause such a smell? Unlikely. The detectors would have set off the alarms. And the Chinese takeout she'd eaten at ten smelled nothing like sweet almonds. Yet, she couldn't deny the odd odor, pleasantly pungent, permeating the room like an enticing cologne.

Listening intently, she heard nothing except the computer humming, the coffee perking and the water cooler cycling on in the dim hallway outside her office door. The elevator had remained silent all evening.

The scent filled her nostrils—a smell that didn't

belong. Fallon set down her papers, glanced at her watch. Ten past midnight. Time to go home. She'd mention the odor to the security guard on the way out.

She stood, reached for her purse and shut down her computer. The air crackled. Reddish sparks sputtered as if someone had set off fireworks, creating an eerie glow on the high-gloss walls, lacquered desk, and smoked mirrors. Fallon almost gagged on the overpowering stench of burning almonds.

Raising her hand to shield her face, she squinted through ruby, vermillion and crimson sparks. Was there an electrical short? Had heat lightning somehow bounced into the office building? She retreated until her backside pressed against the glass pane overlooking Tampa Bay. Just what the hell was going on?

Right before her astonished eyes, a man's black silhouette emerged amidst starlike bursts of streaking light. She blinked hard. Where had he come from? One moment she'd been alone, the next, as if her thoughts had summoned him, he'd appeared out of nowhere. Scarlet surges of electricity zapped his barrel-like chest, zigzagged down his wide-spread legs, smoked beneath his black boots. The intruder stood unaffected by the energy spattering around him and ignored the smoke spiraling about his feet.

Fallon rocked back on her heels, stunned by his astounding arrival. Who was he? What was he? Perhaps his strange clothing shielded him, but she wore no such protection. Before the electric energy could shock her, she dashed toward the door, but tripped on a lamp cord, and bumped into an end table, spilling a box of Godiva chocolates. She sprawled across the floor, dropping her purse, scattering the contents, including her gun and cell phone, which skidded out of reach under the credenza. He could have her wallet, her credit cards, her jewelry and her gun—as long as she got away from the zapping electricity…and him.

Scrambling on her knees toward the office door, she looked behind her—but he'd disappeared. How odd. She had no idea where he was hiding and didn't stop to look. However, her office didn't offer many possibilities to conceal a man of his height. As long as he stayed out of sight, she could keep hoping she wouldn't need to employ her rusty hand-to-hand combat skills, especially against a man so powerfully built.

She moved forward, toward the only exit—and saw him standing directly in her path, his black seamless boots blocking her escape. She swallowed down her surprise and climbed to her feet, looking up. The sparks had disappeared, and there was nothing out of the ordinary in the rest of the room—no fire, no blackened ceiling, no smoke. Even the burning scent was disappearing quickly.

She focused on the man. A glimmering black faceplate, set flush in a helmet that covered his face, gave him the appearance of leaning aggressively forward. A strange one-piece garment constructed of black shiny material strained over the rest of him, outlining every muscle.

She didn't recognize his uniform, but she recognized the type. Military. A specialist. And if she hadn't been notified of his appearance, he couldn't be CIA—not unless the Agency had royally screwed up. And if he wasn't one of them, he had to be the enemy.

Not even her CIA training had prepared her for these circumstances. Working the party crowd was much more her speed—not bumping into mysterious men in black who arrived unannounced in a shower of sparks in the middle of the night.

He folded his arms across his chest. "What are you doing here?"

She wasn't buying into his controlled, I-won't-hurt-you attitude. His voice vibrated with life, yet sounded both warm and resigned, and she couldn't place the accent. Since he'd asked why she was in her own office, he obviously didn't recognize her, a definite point in her favor. Hopefully, he'd have no idea of her secret work for the Agency. And if he didn't know she controlled one of the largest fortunes in the United States, she had no intention of enlightening him.

"I was just leaving."

She edged toward the door. She didn't know how the man had sneaked past security, or where the sparks had come from, or why the electricity hadn't killed him. Only a man with superpowers or superior technology could have withstood such high voltage. While he more than looked the part of futuristic superhero—the body beneath that form-fitting material rivaled Brad Pitt's—he was blocking her exit and she wanted out—now. She tingled from head to foot even though the electricity had long since disappeared and she wondered if that scent could have drugged her. Nevertheless she sidled three more steps toward the door. Perhaps her nerves were simply warning her of danger—a very dangerous attraction to the stranger, which had her questioning her sanity.

Fallon must have blinked because he suddenly blocked her path again. She never saw him take a step, never heard a footfall. No one could move so fast and yet… That almond scent must have drugged her. She had to be hallucinating. And she certainly shouldn't be so aware of his attractive body, those wide shoulders that didn't quit, his tapered torso and powerful arms.

"Is it after midnight?" A tinge of confusion colored his tone, but perhaps it was just the helmet muffling his voice. He wasn't necessarily a terrorist. Perhaps he'd escaped from a mental institution and that explained the strange clothing. Or he might be a thief after one of their highly classified research projects.

Humor him. Stall for time. Ignore the sizzling electrical charge through your veins.

She glanced at her watch. "It's twelve-twenty."

His broad shoulders stiffened. "And the date?"

Refusing to let him draw her into small chat, she sidestepped away once more. "My money and credit cards are in my wallet. Take what you want." *And let me go.*

"You were not supposed to be here. It's inconvenient."

Fallon gave him an incredulous frown. "Excuse me. You find it inconvenient that I'm working in *my* office?"

"You will make my work more difficult."

His work? She wondered exactly what that was, but now wasn't the time for a chat. If he thought of her as an obstacle he might be glad to be rid of her. She tried not to think of his alternative to letting her go.

"I'll pretend I never saw you."

He shook his head. "You will remain with me. You need a vacation—"

"Vacation?" It took a moment for his statement to register. "You heard my conversation?" She gasped, more alarmed than embarrassed. How could he have been in the room without Fallon noticing while she'd spoken to Jaycee?

"Perhaps I'm the man you need to fill your fantasy." The disembodied voice coming from behind the black faceplate unnerved her. She had yet to see his face and at his personal comment alarm zinged down her spine.

But when he again blocked her path, speaking in a slightly stilted way as if English was not his native tongue, her breath lodged in her throat. She hadn't seen him move. He was simply just there, in her way, preventing escape.

Suddenly, the faceplate in his helmet disappeared. One instant his features were covered and the next his face was bared. He stared at her with eyes as black as a midnight sky shimmering with bright stars. For a moment they held her captive. Then finally she let out her breath, relieved he was…human. And, oh, was he human, with his bold nose and arrogant brows and cheekbones to die for. Though the tension still churned in her gut, she found those human features reassuring. Somehow his enigmatic entrance into her office had caused her to conjure images of aliens and monsters behind the faceplate, not compelling eyes that softened the harsh high cheekbones, thin lips curling into a sexy grin and an expression of curiosity that stimulated her imagination when it should have increased her wariness.

Reminding herself that bad guys could have pretty faces, she forced her legs into motion, lurched around him and sprinted through the doorway. At the speed he moved, at any moment, she expected him to jerk her to a halt. As she rounded the first corner and headed for the red exit sign above the staircase, she didn't dare risk a glance back.

Her heart raced. Her palms dampened with sweat as she shoved against the heavy stairwell door. It swung open, and she lunged into the murky hallway.

Not too fast.

Don't fall.

As she dashed down the steps, she listened for the creak of the metal door opening behind her and a sign of pursuit. Nothing.

Good. The Black Marauder must have wanted her

wallet after all. Rushing down another flight, she wondered if she dared stop and take the elevator.

While she debated, inexplicable, unnatural icy chills suddenly washed over her. But she ignored her shivers, obviously an aftershock resulting from her previous adrenaline rush.

She wasn't yet safe, she reminded herself. If the intruder took the elevator with the intention of intercepting her somewhere between this floor and the lobby, she should exit the stairwell on one of the lower floors to avoid him. Perhaps she should try to make it to another phone to call 911 but the other offices would likely be locked, and although she could pick a lock, she was way out of practice. As Fallon considered her options, she fled down the third flight.

Her stomach suddenly cramped with nausea, knocking her to her knees. Fallon had been frightened before. This sensation was intensely different. Dizziness engulfed her in a vortex. Only a fierce grip on the banister kept her from plunging headfirst to the concrete landing.

Her heart pounded like a jackhammer in her chest, and she fought back the blackness of a faint. Unable to go on, even if her life depended on it, she collapsed to a sitting position on a step, barely maintaining the presence of mind to lower her head between her knees.

Fallon wasn't prone to illness or fainting. In fact, she'd barely missed a day of school due to sickness. She'd never experienced anything like this and hoped she never would again.

"You will feel completely better in a few minutes," he said with a thread of concern in his tone.

At his voice, she jerked up her head. He was standing beside her, his gaze sympathetic, as if he cared about her plight. Where had he come from? He seemed to have appeared out of nowhere. Splitting pain from the sudden motion of turning her head caused her to moan. Damn. She knew better than to reveal weakness. But her head felt like an army was marching through it.

He extended an arm toward her, a damp paper towel in his hand, almost as if he'd known in advance how ill she'd be feeling. "Put this on your forehead."

She dabbed the cool napkin on her heated face and neck, head aching too much to think past his inexplicable behavior, both kind and eerie. How had he known in advance she would require care? What motivated him to try to ease the discomfort? Despite the questions reverberating in her mind, she was grateful when her physical woes eased with the surprising speed he'd predicted. Her stomach settled. If only she could get her spinning thoughts in order.

Who was this guy? He'd sneaked into her office, eavesdropped on her private conversation and not only did he move faster than her eyes could focus, he'd anticipated her sudden illness and foreseen her seemingly miraculous recovery.

He spoke gently as if he understood her brain was tender from the strange illness. "For your own good, you must accept that I mean you no harm and—"

"For my own good?"

"Every time you leave me, the illness will strike."

"Excuse me?" The man was certifiable. A body of steel and a mind of mush. She would have screamed if she'd thought her tender head could take it. Instead, she spoke with care. "I don't want to stay with you."

"You have no choice." While warmth and regret colored his voice, the gaze that swept over her was nothing short of intensely interested. He shot her a charming smile. "You belong with me now."

Oh God! She wasn't buying into his cute dimples. A crazy man had claimed her for his own. But at least he didn't sound as if he intended to kill her. And while she lived she had a chance to escape. Or call for help. But how?

His idea that fleeing his presence could have caused the nausea she'd just suffered was absurd. As the sickening dizziness faded, her thoughts raced. Never before had she endured such disabling queasiness. Perhaps it was the strange almond scent that had sickened her. The few times she'd suffered from sea sickness, the illness had come on gradually and disappeared slowly. What she'd just experienced had hit as fast and hard as a speeding truck. Just as odd was her quick recovery.

Glancing at the man, she searched for clues to his identity and character. There were no marks of identification to relieve the unremitting blackness of his strange suit, no badges, no lettering, no insignia. And by the way he stretched the limits of the material, he clearly hid nothing in a pocket.

Despite that his words made no sense, she couldn't deny the intelligent compassion in his eyes, and she had the feeling he would have liked to take her into his arms to comfort her but sensed his touch would alarm her.

His sheer size tended to dominate the area around him, but his voice remained gentle, almost soothing. "Fallon, it's time we leave here."

We?

She looked into his black eyes and wondered why she didn't feel more threatened. As she listened to the thread of determination in his tone, it seemed prudent to humor him. While she wasn't certain what would happen if she refused to cooperate, she didn't think this was a good time to find out. If he knocked her unconscious, she couldn't fight back. With no one in the building except the guard downstairs, a scream for help was unlikely to be heard. So, she stood, straightening her suit jacket, and gazed into his mesmerizing black eyes. She would try to gain information.

"How did you know my name?"

His arm swung out, her purse dangling from his index finger. She grabbed it, but didn't bother checking the contents for her weapon. She already knew from the weight that he hadn't returned her gun, but from the expression in his eyes as much as his patient demeanor she'd already decided that petty thievery was beneath him. She figured that after rifling through her wallet he'd learned her name.

Wariness of his motives gripped her, but she hesitated to run from him again. The memory of that sudden illness was too sharp just yet to try again. Besides, at the speed he moved, he could easily catch her.

Damn! What did he want? Why did he stand so close, looming over her as if he feared she might collapse and he'd have to catch her. She imagined those big arms scooping her up, gathering her against his chest and wondered what was wrong with her. She should be assessing the danger, gathering intel, not sizing him up as a man.

She needed to find out exactly what he was after. Obviously, he didn't mean to kill her—or he'd already have done so.

She lifted her chin and rocked back on her heels. "Who are you?"

He fired a wicked grin at her. "My name is not important."

"Then what is?"

"We don't have time for explanations right now. I need to watch television. Where is the one in your office?"

"It's being serviced."

"Do you have one at home?"

Just when he'd convinced her of his intelligence, he said something so wacko she was back to thinking he'd escaped from the loony bin. While she wanted to leave the stairwell and go down to the ground floor where she might possibly find some help, she didn't want to bring him to her home.

Yet lying to him about the television didn't seem

like a good idea, either. "Yes. I have television but the cable is out."

He raised his brow as if in disbelief that both her televisions required repairs. But then he shrugged. "I'll fix it."

Before she exhaled, she found herself standing next to her car in the parking garage. How could it be? One moment she'd stood on the stairwell in her office building and the next instant she found herself twenty stories lower, having somehow crossed through tons of steel and concrete. She had no memory of walking down the stairs, taking the elevator or going through the lobby where she'd intended to call out for help.

Shaken, Fallon faced the unperturbed stranger over the hood of her car. "How did you do that?"

"Do what?"

"How did we get from upstairs to down here," she snapped her fingers, "like that?"

2

"I TOLD YOU that I have no time for explanations."
Seemingly all business, he didn't hesitate to open her
purse, dig out the car keys and toss them to her.
"Drive."

She wanted to demand answers but didn't think
irritating him would be prudent. Not in her circumstances. Somehow he'd neatly whisked her past the
security guard, her last hope for rescue. Her instincts
screamed a warning not to go off alone with him, but
the deserted parking garage was not the place for another escape attempt. While she'd recovered completely from the nausea, now with her full attention
on him, she sensed an urgency within him, indicated
by the ticking muscle in his neck, the tightness of his
jaw and the occasional fisting of his fingers. And she
wondered if he'd turn violent if provoked.

Yet she didn't think he meant her harm. Common
sense told her if he'd meant to rape or murder her,
he'd have already done so. It also seemed odd to her
that he'd asked her to drive. He was obviously a man
accustomed to taking charge, so for him to ask her
to drive seemed out of character. But then nothing

made sense right now, not his strange appearance, not her peculiar illness, not the impossible way they'd traveled to the parking garage.

"Why don't you just whisk us straight to my home? Why bother to drive?"

He glanced to the right, then the left. "I need to orient myself."

"Orient yourself to what?"

"Come on." He ignored her question. "Let's go."

Her hands trembled as she unlocked her car. He ducked his head and folded himself into the passenger seat. As Fallon started the car and shifted into reverse, he opened the glove compartment and unfolded her Tampa map.

If he were a stranger to the city, perhaps she could drive straight to the police station. She recalled the closest office was on Jackson Street, but she couldn't remember which one-way street to take. Unwilling to kindle his suspicion by making an accidental wrong turn, she decided to hop on the Crosstown Expressway and head for the Brandon sheriff's office near her home. It might be farther, but she wouldn't get lost.

Using her flashlight, he studied the map, then flipped it over and perused the Brandon side for a minute before refolding it on the creases and neatly replacing the items. He stared straight ahead, his eyes distant and unreadable, appearing to be a man with a lot on his mind.

But what was going on behind the dark eyes and charming smile? Was he planning criminal acts? Terrorist acts? He'd given her so few clues that she couldn't begin to make an educated guess and that unnerved her as much as the personal danger. Fallon was accustomed to taking charge to solve problems—but if she couldn't discern what he was planning, she couldn't come up with a plan to counter him. Her frustration soared. Patience was not one of her best qualities.

Despite the lack of traffic on the road at this hour, she drove with uncharacteristic slowness past Harbor Island and Garrison Channel. Driving through the growing city and admiring the changes from seedy warehouses to shiny tourist destinations usually gave Fallon hope. She'd relocated the research institute's headquarters from New York five years ago, believing the Florida climate would attract the world's top researchers. And she'd been right. Thanks to her perseverance, a few tax concessions from the county commissioners, the Hanover money and several brilliant technologists, Fallon believed before the end of the decade they would find a cure for cancer.

Pushing the thought of business away, she concentrated on the passenger beside her, who remained unnaturally still and silent until she glided over a low spot in the road.

"What is that smell?" he asked.

Between his need to consult a map and his curiosity over the smell of swamp and sewage, she assumed he was a stranger to the area, but she wanted to be certain before she drove to the sheriff's office. "You've never noticed it before?"

He shrugged.

She sighed and wondered why she ever thought squeezing information from him would be possible. The man wasn't talkative. He hadn't even told her his name.

The road to Brandon was a straight shot east and only a few pairs of headlights broke through the darkness. In contrast to the modern highway, abandoned warehouses and rusting fences lurked in the shadows beyond the occasional streetlight.

She exited from the expressway onto Highway 60, Brandon's main road. A few more minutes and she'd reach the sheriff's office. Trying not to fidget or turn her head, she passed the turnoff to her home.

"You missed your street." Her passenger swiveled and raised a speculative eyebrow.

She'd underestimated him. How had he known? She ignored him, driving straight ahead, with a brazenness she didn't feel. "I did?"

"Turn around." His voice cut the air with a steely edge.

She made a U-turn with a sinking sensation in the pit of her chest. Perhaps she should jump out of the car at the light. Make a run for it. Only the light stayed green, damn it, and she couldn't work up the courage to deliberately crash into a telephone pole or a ditch. If the car flipped, she'd die along with him.

As if he read her thoughts, he reached over and locked her door, then strapped the safety belt over her lap.

"What are you doing?" She couldn't prevent her voice from rising an octave.

"Calm yourself. An accident would be inconvenient."

"Not to mention we could die."

"Dying would be inconvenient," he agreed in a breezy tone and with an amused smile, as if he hadn't understood her wry humor. "Turn right, then left."

Could he read her mind? Or had he investigated her ahead of time? But if he knew her address, then why had he scanned the map? "How do you know where I live?"

The helmet covering the rest of his head disappeared, and he raked a hand through his short, dark hair. "Your driver's license. And the map."

He'd barely glanced at the map, never mind plotted a route and memorized the street names, which made her believe he'd planned more than he admitted. And she wasn't even going to think about where his helmet had disappeared to. She'd always known her wealth made her a target, but the man hadn't mentioned ransom or extortion. He hadn't threatened her, hadn't touched her. Yet sooner or later the matter of her money would come up—it always did. And the sooner she knew how much it would cost her to get rid of him, the sooner she'd know where she stood.

"What do you want with me?"

"Not a damn thing." He gave her another one of those charming smiles. "But it looks like I'm stuck with you."

His assumption that *he* was stuck with *her* struck a nerve. He'd invaded her office and had kidnapped her and now he was complaining that he was stuck with her? Irritated, she took a corner fast and the tires squealed, gripping the loose gravel of the side street.

"Pull the car over."

"Why?"

"Do it."

Fallon slowed on the dark, deserted street, wondering if her driving had frightened him—but he didn't appear to be a man who worried about fast speeds. The crescent moon vanished behind somber clouds. He shifted impatiently in his seat, and when he unlocked his door, the click sent an alarming shiver through her. She had to remind herself that he'd had opportunities to harm her before now and hadn't taken them.

After she pulled to a complete stop, she sat frozen behind the wheel, her fingers clenched around the seat belt. He hadn't asked her to turn off the motor. As he opened his door, she considered whether to throw the car in Drive the moment he stepped out, but he remained in the seat and turned to her.

"When I exit this vehicle, drive slowly toward your house."

Like hell, she'd drive slowly. If he didn't move out of the way, she'd run him over.

"Drive slowly," he repeated, sounding as if he cared about her, "or the sickness will make you so ill you won't recover until morning."

He slipped out of the car and shut the door. Her

hand slammed down and locked him out. She pressed her foot on the accelerator. Why he freed her, she had no idea, but she didn't hesitate to take advantage of her good fortune.

She had no intention of driving home, where he could jog down the block and recapture her. She'd retrace her route and head straight to the sheriff's office.

But recalling her former illness, she didn't press the pedal to the floor as she would have liked. She kept her velocity to only ten miles over the speed limit. Before she'd driven half a block, nausea smacked her with the force of a head-on collision. Tidal waves of dizziness returned, pummeling her head, squeezing her breath from her lungs, twisting her stomach into knots.

Fallon hit the brakes and gasped. What had he done to her? Could he have somehow hypnotized her?

Her body screamed for relief. Through her pain, she remembered how his proximity eased the horrible nausea. She threw the car into Reverse.

Suddenly he sat beside her, inside the car. One moment he'd been gone, the next he rode in the passenger seat as if he'd never left. Once again she slammed on the brakes, thankful for the seat belt that kept her from smashing into the steering wheel. Was she crazy? Hallucinating? Drugged?

"Are you all right?"

She drew deep breaths and didn't bother responding to the sympathy in his tone. Just as they had earlier, the violent sensations subsided. He remained silent, allowing her to recover and finally she raised her head, eyeing him with suspicion.

"I'm better now," she admitted.

Before she'd worried how to escape this man. Now she bit into her bottom lip concerned *he* might leave *her.* She could never withstand this intense physical agony for more than a few moments.

"It's going to get worse." His words rang with regret.

She turned her head slowly to look at him, horror clutching her throat tight. "Worse?"

"The comfort distance between us will shrink." His tone softened with pity, as if he wished he could change whatever the hell he was doing to her. "Eventually you will not be able to take more than a step or two from my side before suffering."

"Suffering from what?"

"The nausea."

"That's not what I meant and you know it. What's causing this illness?" He stared straight ahead. She hated silence more than anything. She hated being kept in the dark. Although the adult Fallon now understood why her parents hadn't told her about her childhood friend's cancer, facts made coping with difficult situations easier. Once she had facts, she could work to fix the problem. When he remained silent, she slapped her palm on the steering wheel. "Look, mister, it's late, I'm tired and in no mood for games."

"You're right." When he agreed with her she

hoped he'd start explaining, but his sympathetic attitude disappeared in a flash. "I don't have time for explanations. Take me to your home. I need to watch television."

She'd feared he might be isolating her because he intended to take advantage of her, and he wished to watch television? "Do you plan to hurt me?"

"Not if I can help it."

"What does that mean?"

"It means—cooperate. And since I'm forced to work with you, you may call me Kane."

"I don't understand."

"Your understanding isn't required. Just do as you're told and we'll get along fine."

The lack of information was driving her anxiety into high gear and she didn't like his domineering attitude. "Suppose I don't want to get along?"

He sighed as if she was being impossible, yet his voice remained gentle and a touch of amusement entered his tone. "If I have time, I will try and be your fantasy man. Will that please you?"

"No," she snapped without hesitation.

"I think I'd enjoy pleasing you."

"Getting to know you that well is not part of any of my plans."

"Sometimes the best-laid plans have to be thrown away." He raised his eyebrow and his mouth quirked up, revealing an attractive dimple. "I heard your conversation with your friend. You want to be swept away. You want to escape your responsibilities." His tone turned personal and his eyes flashed with a spark of heat. "And what man could resist such an intriguing idea?"

She spoke with care, through gritted teeth, her alarm soaring right along with her interest. Why couldn't she have met this fascinating man under less bizarre circumstances? She knew nothing about him and yet…she could feel a nameless connection forming between them that sizzled on a sexual level. "Surely, you understand the difference between fantasy and reality."

His eyes glinted with intrigue and heat. "Are you so lost that you don't think fantasies can come true?"

His tone suggested that she was the crazy one. And this turn of conversation was striking way too close. Because fantasies didn't come true, not hers. And she should be drawing information out of her abductor, not discussing her fantasy life with him—a man she found way too attractive.

The combination of his sympathy for her plight, amusement when she gave him attitude and obvious intelligence was lowering her guard. He was getting to her in a way she'd never believed possible. He seemed so intent on his goal and yet she had the impression that although she stood in his way, he didn't intend to harm her. But she had to remain wary. Since he didn't seem inclined to believe anything she said, she decided the safest course right then was to remain silent.

He turned the radio on, and the strains of a Garth Brooks ballad filled the car, hindering further conversation. Not that Fallon considered lack of conversation with this "Kane" a great loss, since he rarely answered her questions, and when he did, he confused her even more.

But she worried about his suggestion, alarmed that he might appoint himself in charge of making her fantasy come true. The idea both frightened and intrigued her. She shouldn't be thinking about his looks or how his eyes had gleamed with warmth when the conversation turned personal. If they'd been together on a CIA mission, she might have gone along with letting him become her fantasy man. But she knew nothing about Kane—except that he used technology she'd never seen before. And yet, she couldn't deny to herself that she felt more alive right at this moment than she had in a very long time.

Logic told her she was responding to more than his great body and his interesting face. The secrecy and power and all his self-control fascinated her. She'd been around enough agents and on enough missions to recognize that high stakes elevated her hormone levels. But under normal circumstances she'd still find Kane interesting. His slight accent and warm tone were seductive. And those dimples. She'd always been a sucker for dimples.

However, she'd never, ever, been turned on by violence or force. The choice had to be hers.

As she drove to her house at the end of the road, she realized he'd left the car to teach her she needed him. The incident on the stairwell could have been coincidence, but the dizzying sensations had now occurred twice, both times when they'd been apart. She shuddered, unwilling to experience them again. Clearly he'd done something to her but that didn't mean she would surrender to his every demand.

Driving through the gate, for the first time, she regretted the privacy of her home. Set back from the road, the location gave her a solitude she usually cherished. Tonight the isolation would work against her. No one would notice the lights burning late. No one would glimpse a strange man through the twelve-foot windows.

Fallon debated whether to trip the security alarm that would summon the police. While the police could stop him from whatever he intended to do with her, suppose the cops separated them and she became ill? No one would believe her. They'd lock her away and she'd suffer horribly. She shuddered. She'd have to deal with this man by herself, figure out how he was making her ill and find a way to stop him.

After opening the garage door with her automatic opener, she turned off the car, and disarmed the security system. She walked into the black-and-white kitchen with its array of plants, herbs and potted flowers to warm the decor. "Home, sweet home."

A home with all the amenities, a screened pool, cathedral ceilings and a phone in every room—including the bathrooms. She'd use her first opportunity to telephone the Agency and notify them of her situation. But would anyone in their right mind believe her?

She gestured toward the entertainment center

in the den. "The television's in there. I'll just go freshen up."

She rounded the corner and walked into the bathroom. After closing the door, she flipped on the light. Believing she was alone, Fallon turned and discovered Kane had zapped himself into the bathroom.

Startled, she gasped. "Why don't you give me a little warning before you do that?"

Kane leaned against the bathroom's far wall and held her telephone, the disconnected cord dangling in one hand, his cocky grin telling her that he enjoyed playing games. "I'll collect the rest of these so you won't be tempted."

"Why? Because telling someone about you would be inconvenient?"

"I'm glad you understand." His austere features broke into a wide smile that revealed straight teeth. In the bright bathroom, she saw that his eyes weren't black, but a deep sapphire-blue. Their gazes met for a moment, and if she wasn't mistaken, he found her attempt to goad him humorous. She couldn't seem to help appreciating his intelligence and the calm way he dealt with her defiance.

Even worse, she was enjoying the electric connection between them that felt more like flirtation than anything dangerous. When he strolled out the door, she refused to shrink back against the sink to avoid contact. His hand lightly brushed her hip, causing pure heat to shoot up into her chest and down to her toes. She clenched the counter for support, determined not to reveal how much his casual touch had affected her, then slumped when she was finally alone.

She had to get a grip. He was not someone she'd chosen to bring home. He'd inserted himself into her night and she had yet to determine how much of a threat he was. She imagined him walking—no, popping—from room to room, disconnecting every phone. She couldn't summon help and couldn't leave without becoming desperately ill. She was a prisoner, stuck with a man she was much too attracted to, a man who had claimed he'd like the job of being her fantasy man, a man who had all the right stuff to carry out that role.

Fallon splashed cold water on her face, reviewing her alternatives. She would not fall prey to Stockholm syndrome, where a victim fell in love with her captor. Realistically, she had only one good option. Upstairs, hidden at the back of her closet lay her best hope. He'd left her no choice. She would have to go for her backup gun.

After cracking open the bathroom door, she watched Kane open the cabinet that held the big television and remove the remote control from atop the cabinet. "It seems to work just fine."

She didn't answer. She slipped off her shoes, then silently ran upstairs. Half expecting that at any moment he'd pop in front of her and tell her to stay with him where he could watch her, she made the most of his distraction with the television.

She padded across the thick carpet. Sweat beaded on her brow. Her heart skipped erratically. She entered her closet and flung aside scarves, gloves and purses, seeking cold metal until she clutched the 9 mm automatic.

With practiced ease, she flipped off the safety, pulled the slide back to chamber the first of nine rounds. She remembered the gun instructor's words like he'd said them yesterday. "Don't go for a weapon unless you intend to shoot. Don't shoot unless you aim to kill."

She'd never fired a gun at anyone, never mind aimed to kill—but she'd never been kidnapped, either. Taking a deep breath, Fallon crept silently down the steps. Kane hunched forward on the leather sofa, staring at the television with a frown of concentration.

She stepped closer, aiming at his chest. "I don't know what you did to me, but I want you to undo it."

Kane raised a brow, his expression one of disappointment rather than fear. "You're in this until the end."

The end? That sounded like a death threat.

"What do you want with me?" she asked, determined to pry information from him.

Ignoring the weapon, he broke into a grin so sexy, it stole her breath. His eyes locked on hers with an intimate look of pure awareness. "I want nothing except what you're willing to give."

"I'm not giving you one damn thing."

The heat in his tone could have melted sugar. "Before we're done, you'll want to put me in charge."

His words seared her like a bolt of lightning and

she fought to ignore the electric charge sizzling up and down her veins.

Despite her gun, she didn't feel in control and her voice hitched. "I'll put you in charge of what?"

"In charge of you." He chuckled, his glance enticing and knowing.

As he stood and advanced toward her, his rhythm steady and decisive, his eyes blazed with a powerful determination and emphatic certainty that she would give him whatever he asked of her.

She would never agree. Never. Even if her breasts tingled with excitement at the thought, even if she felt a sudden swooping pull in her belly at the idea of allowing him to do with her as she wished. As if sensing the conflict between her thoughts and her physical needs, he let his eyes drop to her breasts where her traitorous nipples had betrayed her by hardening into tight buds. He smiled knowingly and with pure pleasure, telling her that he most definitely liked what he was seeing.

"You do want me," his tone coaxed. "The idea of giving yourself over to me excites you, doesn't it?"

"You are so wrong," she denied while recalling that he'd overheard much more of her conversation with Jaycee. Too bad Jaycee was right and she really did need a good fantasy to sweep her away. She hadn't taken a vacation in years. Hadn't had a fling in longer than she cared to remember. And Kane was perfect in so many ways, polite, yet in charge, intelligent and charming. She would love to ditch her responsibilities and just play. In fact, the idea was so appealing that if she knew for certain Kane wouldn't hurt her, she'd toss the gun aside and let him have her.

"Deny me all you like." His gaze swept over her flushed face and lingered on her lips, lips that suddenly burned for a kiss. "Your body tells a different story." He advanced another step, his eyes telling her oh-so clearly that he wanted her. "Imagine giving over complete control to me. You will have no decisions to make, no choices. Just the freedom to enjoy whatever I decide."

"No." The protest came out automatically, but his words shot heat straight to her core. He was a stranger. He'd kidnapped her.

"Yes," he insisted.

In another step, he'd be close enough to disarm her.

And Fallon pulled the trigger.

3

IN THE SMALL ROOM the shot sounded as loud as a cannon and the scent of powder burned her nostrils. If he hadn't egged her on, she might not have found the courage to pull the trigger. His words had been too enticing, too tempting and for a moment she'd feared yielding to him more than she feared taking a life. He'd gotten to her with his sexy smile, hot eyes and compelling promise of taking away all her responsibilities by fulfilling her fantasy. Only she'd never fantasized about giving up control of herself. That was his interpretation and she wasn't buying it for a second. So what if her body had turned on at his words? Or that the heat in his gaze was real? She liked reading about crossing the country in a covered wagon but that didn't mean she wanted to do it. She enjoyed watching ski jumping at the Olympics but that didn't mean she wanted to try it. So maybe his words made her insides go all mushy, but she was way too strong-willed to turn over her will to him— no matter how badly she wanted a vacation.

So she'd pulled the trigger and kept her eyes wide open, expecting to have to steal herself for the sight of blood and mangled flesh. But Kane was gone and she couldn't prevent a shiver of relief that he'd pulled his dematerialization trick again.

He couldn't have gone too far, or she'd be sick. Fallon extended the gun in both hands and spun, searching for her target. She held her breath and listened, but only the whisper of a breeze ruffling the miniblinds and the clock ticking above the convection oven interrupted the haunting silence.

Every female instinct told her to throw down the gun and agree to an exciting fling. Yet her mind told her he was dangerous. She couldn't leave so she had no choice but to stay and fight. Too bad she was spending so much effort fighting her own desires.

How had a connection arced between them so quickly? Even as she searched for him she already knew he wouldn't be angry. Another man would be furious that she'd tried to shoot him, but not Kane. He seemed to understand her fears—of him, of herself, of what might happen between them if she let it.

As a trained agent, she could ignore her attraction. And his. No matter how enticing she found his heat, she couldn't succumb to an absolute stranger.

She longingly eyed the phones he'd collected and piled on the glass dining table. Dare she take a moment to plug one in and call the Agency for help? But even if a fellow CIA agent arrived, he would never believe the truth. She imagined what kind of reaction she'd receive after she described a man who moved faster than the eye could see, a man who made her desperately ill when she tried to escape from him. A man who thought she would give him everything he asked for. A man who thought she would put him in charge of her.

Kane might not have specified his exact intention, but the heat in his gaze had clued her into the notion that he aimed to dominate her physically, sexually, mentally—and he actually had the conceit to expect her to agree.

At the thought, her hands shook. Because his idea so appealed. What woman wouldn't want to put herself in the hands of a man like Kane and accept all the pleasure he could give? And for her the allure was all the more intriguing because she was so tired of being the one in charge. Her family depended on her. Her corporations and charities depended on her. For once it would be terrific to give up her responsibilities and just go with the flow. Her mind might be denouncing the idea of ever yielding to him, but her body was reacting favorably. Despite the connection that had grown between them, no way was she putting her hormones in charge.

Turning, searching for him, she sensed his nearness by the strange link they shared. He was close, inside the house. Recalling his special abilities and his speed of movement increased the beat of her heart until blood hammered in her ears. She might have the gun, but he stalked her like prey.

His arms suddenly enfolded her and slammed her back against his hard chest.

"No!"

"Yes." He whispered the word into her ear like a dangerous caress.

He trapped her between his arms and his chest and, reaching forward, seized her gun with his powerful hands. She'd tried to kill him and logic told her that he would turn the weapon on her. Logic said she was going to die, and she distantly wished she'd spent a little more time on her own happiness. She should have gone skiing with Jaycee. She should have taken a trip to Hawaii. She should have…

Fallon clenched her hands tight. God! She wanted to live, but she would not beg. Closing her eyes, she held her breath and waited for the blast of a shot. And death.

And yet feminine instinct told her this man meant her no harm. Female instinct told her he admired her courage. And deep down she knew he wanted her too much to kill her.

"If you really feel safer with this gun in your hands," his expression remained gentle, "you may have it back."

After showing her that she couldn't shoot him and that he could disarm her at will, she understood that handing her back the gun was a mere gesture. The gun was useless against him. With her back pressed against his chest, his breath fanning her ear, it took her a moment to focus on the important part of his statement.

"Why the hell do you care if I feel safe?" She tilted back her head and caught his charged gaze, one electric enough to light up her every nerve.

He frowned at her, but even his frown was sexy and superior. "Your fear is complicating my mission."

"Which is what exactly?"

KANE RELEASED HER, letting her keep the gun. "I'm not yet at liberty to reveal that data. However, if you'd allow me to watch television for ten uninterrupted minutes, I could…" He couldn't say more. His orders were to reveal his mission to no one.

And he couldn't blame her for the suspicion in her eyes. But she wasn't supposed to have been in her office and now he was stuck with her—although he didn't know if stuck was the right way to describe having to remain close to a beautiful, intelligent woman. After overhearing her conversation, he'd felt so attuned to her. And then he'd gone and frightened her to the point that she'd tried to kill him.

From the moment he'd arrived in her office, she'd seemed wary, but in spite of the incomprehensible things happening to her, she'd remained calm and together. However, she hadn't been totally able to hide her attraction to him. Oh, she'd fooled him, procuring her backup weapon, but he couldn't miss the relief in her sagging shoulders after she'd fired the shot and missed.

So much like him, duty was calling her to do one thing, when desire demanded another. That this wealthy businesswoman would try to shoot him had taken him by complete surprise. His second mistake, no doubt due to how she kept distracting him.

Her short dark hair framed her attractive face in pixielike curls that disguised her cunning. Her slenderness gave an appearance of fragility that had deceived and attracted him. And the feminine curve of her hips in the tight skirt diverted him from remembering Fallon Hanover ran a multimillion dollar conglomerate. And she'd defended herself as deftly as she ran the Institute.

Although she'd handled the gun proficiently, from the expression of horror when she'd pulled the trigger, he'd bet she'd never before fired with the intent to kill. If he wasn't careful, her combination of strength, determination and foolhardiness could botch his mission, and if he didn't assuage her suspicions, there was no telling what other crazy scheme she'd come up with. However, he wasn't permitted to tell her anything—at least not without permission.

"You could have killed me," he said, hoping that if he stayed firm, she'd pull back and he'd find her less seductive. Kane liked strong women, women who knew what they wanted—but this wasn't the time or the place for a dalliance. And he didn't enter relationships lightly, not after his past disaster. So as appealing as he found Fallon, his talk about becoming her fantasy man had been a joke—one that had taken of a life on its own in his imagination.

"Shooting you would have been self-defense."

She didn't back down an inch and he had to stop himself from applauding. Any way he looked at her, Fallon Hanover was one hell of a woman. And he'd most definitely like to know her better.

Perhaps coming to her home had compounded his mistake. He'd allowed her the advantage of the home ground, giving her options he couldn't anticipate. But if he'd taken her to a public hotel, there was too much risk of a stranger noticing something odd. His enemies could read newspaper headlines for leads, notice that Fallon Hanover had disappeared, and put the facts together.

Her lakeside home had seemed the best option. A pile of unfolded laundry on the couch indicated she didn't expect company. She lived here alone, without servants.

When he'd tried to give her space to adjust to her situation, she'd taken the offensive and her action was forcing him to reassess her. He couldn't drag her around and expect blind cooperation. A woman like her needed answers.

Perhaps her unwillingness to be a victim had altered his opinion of her. Or perhaps holding her in his arms, breathing in the vanilla scent of her hair, watching her rapid pulse beat at the hollow of her neck, feeling her firm bottom wriggling against his thighs had made him realize that his teasing to become her fantasy man had been more than a pleasant diversion to keep her distracted.

Yet in his line of work, civilians were a hindrance. His duty was too important to let anyone distract him. Billions of lives were at stake.

Yet while Fallon would slow him and interfere with his mission, he admitted to himself that he would savor every delicious moment. Despite his attraction to her, if he could have left her behind and gone on with his job alone, he would have. He was caught like a fly in a web—and if he wasn't careful, she'd have him for supper.

From the moment he'd accepted the assignment, the mission had been pure disaster. His briefing had been too sketchy, the timing off, the planning poor. Already his chance of success had been cut by a factor of four, and he'd calculated those odds without figuring in Fallon and his attraction to her. Even worse, he'd violated his sacred vows, mistakenly allowing her to see things she'd had no right to. He'd have to backtrack and feed her lies, convincing lies.

When Kane released her, she spun to face him, her green eyes spitting poisoned daggers that made him want to stroke her like a frightened kitten. She straightened her skirt and, white-faced, glared at him.

He wished he could kiss the distrust off her face, cup the delicate chin, explore her smooth complexion with the pad of his thumb. Her look said she needed explanations, something he didn't have time for. Still, he'd have to justify certain actions or she might attack him again. Not that she could hurt him, but he couldn't jeopardize his work. The greatest danger lay in drawing unwanted attention to himself or in allowing himself to become too fascinated by her.

"Come." He held out his hand to her. "Let's sit in front of the television for a few minutes."

Clutching the gun in one hand, she warily placed her other in his. "Fine."

Clearly, she didn't trust him, but at least she wasn't running screaming from the room, and her hand felt damn good in his. They entered the den together and he turned up the television's volume. Then he removed his watch, which concealed a special transmitter and receiver. The moment he began to transmit, data flashed on his screen.

Fallon leaned over, her scent wafting to his nostrils and teasing him. "What language is that?"

"It's code." Data streamed in about Fallon. "You're CIA?"

He had to give her credit. She didn't change expression. "I run the Hanover Institute."

She might be willing to sink millions into charity to search for a cure for cancer, but she also was no pushover. And at his mention of his knowledge about her, she'd instantly become defensive.

"And you don't simply run the Hanover Institute, you also control a vast personal wealth, don't you?"

As he mentioned her wealth, her eyes darkened, as if mentioning her assets caused her to draw into herself.

"Is that what you want, money?" Her tone sounded resigned, cool and, perhaps, disappointed.

"Your money might prove useful to me, but that's not what I really want." He let his gaze rake over her, and she thought she might tell him to go to hell, but she flicked her tongue over her bottom lip as if considering the full implications of his statement.

While he'd spoken with her, through his transmitter he'd asked his superiors for permission to tell her the truth. As a government agent, surely she could be trusted with secrets. But much to his disappointment, the reply came back: a resounding *No*. He was not allowed to reveal the truth and he was beginning to wonder if he could lie well enough to fool Fallon Hanover, especially after she'd seen the technology he carried.

However, he would try. As his stomach rumbled, reminding him that he needed sustenance, he rose to his feet and brought her to the kitchen, his mind racing.

"So you use the television to transmit and receive messages?" she guessed.

"Sit down. We need to talk."

She cast him a puzzled look and seated herself at the table while he explored the cupboards, pulling out crackers, olives and a jar of caviar. They would both need their strength for what lay ahead. He grabbed a bottle of Chablis, provolone cheese and seedless red grapes from the refrigerator, then returned for two wineglasses and set them on the table.

After filling her glass, he raised his in a toast. "To life."

"I won't be toyed with. If you intend to kill me, just get it over with," she snapped.

"Look, I owe you an apology."

"I'd say you owe me much more than an apology." Her breasts heaved beneath the swell of her silk shirt and when she caught his glance, she frowned—but her nipples hardened. Lovely. Ms. Fallon Hanover

was definitely more interested than she pretended
and he'd have to double his efforts not to become en-
twined in her allure.

But he wasn't adverse to pleasing her—as long as
she didn't slow him down, and as long as she didn't
mind that his emotions would never be involved.
The idea of her totally submitting her will to him excited him. But first he had to assuage her suspicions.

He softened his voice and pointedly raked his gaze
over her. "What kind of apology did you have in
mind?"

Just as he'd planned, his seductive teasing sent
her temper soaring. Her shoulders stiffened. At the
same time, she lowered her lids but not before he'd
glimpsed her response. An angry opponent was not
a smart opponent. Right now he needed her off
balance.

Would she lash out? Try to slap his face? He
should have known she'd have much better control.
She took his attempt to manipulate her in stride, and
he could only admire her tenacity.

"You owe me an explanation of your criminal activities."

"I am not—"

"A crook?"

As she repeated Nixon's famous denial, a spark
of amusement lit her eyes. A twitch pulled at his
lips, and he almost smiled. Fallon was having quite
an effect on his sense of humor as well as an impact
on other parts of him. She'd put him on notice that
she wasn't a woman to trifle with. He couldn't help

wondering if she made love with the same vigor with which she defended herself.

He offered her a glass of wine. "Truce?"

Fallon frowned at it suspiciously and refused his offer. Instead she took the one he'd just sipped from. "Have you drugged me?"

He grinned inside where Fallon couldn't see it. The risks were too great to tell her the truth, and she'd just given him the lead he'd been searching for to set up a convincing lie. "Drugging you wasn't intentional. You were not supposed to be in that office."

Her fingers twisted around the glass stem, sliding up and down. His mouth went cottony dry, thinking how those hands would feel skimming over his neck, his chest, his stomach and lower. Damn it! Not now.

Dragging his thoughts back to the subject at hand, he concentrated on her inquisitive words. "The drug causes hallucinations?"

"Do you recall the scent of almonds?" When she nodded, he continued. "You inhaled the drug. Its side effects are similar but not identical to LSD. Time is distorted and certain memories are forgotten."

Her eyes, green as the potted palm plants swaying in the breezeway, darted to meet his. "That's why I can't remember walking from the stairwell to the parking garage?"

"Exactly."

"And the drug's side effect makes me sick?"

"Yes."

Her full lips thinned into a cynical smile. "But why am I sick only when I leave you?"

"I can't tell you that." Kane spread caviar onto a cracker, popped it onto his tongue and washed the salty-crispness away with a sip of wine.

"Why not?"

Because he couldn't think up a good answer. "It's classified."

"Really?" She raised a delicate eyebrow. "What government do you work for?"

"I can't tell you that either."

"Great. I feel much better now. You won't let me call the police. You won't tell me who you work for." She was ticking off her points on each finger. "You won't tell me why I'm sick. Do you really expect me to believe you?"

Kane leaned forward and held her gaze, assessing her anger. At the radiant flush on her face, the inquisitive gleam in her eye, and the haughty tilt of her chin, admiration welled up and his heart squeezed like a vise. For an instant he regretted what he must do to her, then sternly reminded himself of the lives at stake. He shouldn't care whether he lied to her or not.

Kane didn't let his sympathy for her break through the hardness in his voice. "How else can you explain the nausea?"

She shot him a frustrated look, clearly unable to account for the strange illness. "How long will the drug's effects last?"

"The hallucinations should be gone soon."

"But?" she prodded.

"Occasional flashbacks will occur, so you should

be prepared for memory lapses. The nausea will continue for some time, I'm afraid."

"How long?"

Kane contained a sigh. He could hardly tell her it would last until he finished his mission. "Days. Maybe weeks. I'm not sure."

Her mouth set in annoyance. "You mean I could be stuck with you for an entire month?"

"Yes." He didn't dare remind her that he could make the time interesting for both of them. Or that the maximum nausea-free distance between them would keep shrinking.

She drummed her nails on the table. "Instead of scaring me to death, why didn't you explain earlier?"

"I tried. You didn't want to listen. So I waited for most of the hallucinogenic effect to wear off."

She still looked skeptical. "Why did you break into my office, Kane?"

He plucked a handful of grapes, and savored the crunchy pulp and the sweet juice running down his throat, thinking the worst was over. He shouldn't have let her see the specialized technology at work, but it didn't matter, not if she thought she'd been hallucinating. If he made another error, she'd think she was having a flashback.

Pleased that he'd covered all the contingencies, he leaned back in his chair. "Someone stole technology from…my people. We want it back."

Seemingly oblivious to what the sight did to him she folded her hands across her chest, tightening the blue silk against the soft curve of her breasts. "Let me get this straight." Skepticism entered her tone. "You didn't come into my office to steal but to recover stolen property?"

"We thought the thief might have tried to sell our technology and where better than to the Hanover Institute? You have the money, the interest and the facilities to check out this type of technology. You might have unknowingly purchased the stolen work."

"Why break in? Why not just ask us?"

"My bosses don't want to draw attention to the problem. If you hadn't been there, I would have checked your files, and you'd have never known I was there."

She rubbed her chin in thought. "Don't you have patents that protect your interests?"

Damn! Must the woman keep poking holes in his story? Fallon Hanover was sharp, he'd give her that. But he was good at this type of evasion. The best. "The government prefers to keep its work private. Patents are a matter of public record and we follow national security guidelines."

"Then you do work for us?"

"I didn't say that." He had to give her credit for neatly trapping him.

"I apologize if my skepticism irritates you. You're probably used to people believing your lies after you drug them and take them hostage."

His hand with the wineglass paused on the way to his lips. "You still don't believe me?"

"So what exactly was stolen?"

"I'm not sure."

"Come on! You broke into my office and you don't even know what you're looking for?"

Kane raised his glass to his mouth and swallowed to cover his grin. She really was an interesting woman when she got past her fear of him. "Nigel James had access to many black projects, top-secret. We aren't certain which ones he copied."

"What makes you think this Nigel will attempt to sell your products to a private individual instead of another government?" she asked, her tone mild, her eyes bright with curiosity. "Assuming he stole them, that is."

"We don't think he has the right contacts. We suspect he stole formulas that have more commercial applications. For example, the suit I'm wearing is one of our latest projects."

Her forehead furrowed. "I remember a helmet on that suit."

She seemed uncertain whether the memory was real. Good. "We fabricated intelligent materials."

"Intelligent materials?"

"Nano materials change shape on the microscopic level. For example, walls will someday contain honeycomb-like layers that upon request would reshape to the space required. Wall tiles would switch patterns at the press of a button. A simple tug would stretch a tabletop into a new shape. Countertops sensing food would form themselves into the correct sized dish. The uses are endless."

"With military applications?"

"That's why your help would be useful."

"Help you? I'll die before I betray my country." She kept her face blank, no doubt wondering how much this "help" was going to cost her in dollars.

"Suppose I gave you my word that you aren't?"

"Your word means nothing to me."

Perhaps he could appeal to the businesswoman in her. "When the time comes, you'll see that the plans do not belong to your government. And to entice you, suppose we make a bargain."

"I'm listening." She exaggerated a yawn, contradicting her words. "Sorry. Go on."

He set down his glass. "It's late. Tomorrow will be time enough for explanations. Why don't you turn in for the night?"

"How could I possibly sleep without hearing your bargain?"

"All right." He kept his tone even, although his excitement leaped. "I'd like your full cooperation and help to catch Nigel and reclaim what he has stolen from my government."

"And in return, what will you do for me?"

"I'll give you your complete fantasy." He held his breath. Her reply mattered to him but he had his emotions under control. He would satisfy her and then walk away.

She sucked in her bottom lip. Her hands shook and she had to put down her wine as if fearing she'd spill it. "Be more specific."

He didn't hold back a wolfish grin. "I'd rather show you. However, once we agree there's no going back. As long as I'm here, we'll do this on my terms."

"And suppose I accept and then change my mind?"

"You won't want to—I'll make certain of that."

She eyed him, her head cocked to the side, clearly interested. Her pulse beat a quick tattoo at her neck. Her eyes dilated slightly, but she held his gaze with a courage that was going to make her ultimate submission such a pleasure. A weak woman was no challenge, but Fallon Hanover was strong and her strength excited him, taunted him, dared him.

Although it was unusual for him to be drawn so quickly to a woman, Fallon was special. Besides, it had been way too long since he'd satisfied the demands of his body. He'd let the past haunt him for too long. It was time for him to let go of his past mistakes—ones he wouldn't repeat. While he yearned to explore the passion that pulsed between them, he would be certain not to engage his emotions. He'd love to maintain strict control over what happened between them. He hadn't known Fallon long enough to become deeply involved and he wouldn't stay long enough for more than a physical fling.

"You're arrogant."

He didn't deny it. He was as certain that he'd catch his thief and place him under custody as he was that their time together would be very erotic, very exotic and very special. "Only because I know I will give you pleasure you've never experienced before. Now we'll begin."

4

"I'LL CONSIDER your bargain," she said, hoping he couldn't hear the desire in her tone, her yen to completely give up control to him. For a change, it would be so lovely not to think or plan or be responsible, just give up all control and let him take over. "But, right now, I think it's time to retire."

It didn't matter how damn sexily he'd couched his words. It didn't matter that she found him exciting or his idea tempting. Damn tempting. What were his intentions? She restrained the urge to drum her fingers on the table, unwilling to reveal her raw nerves. Instead, she watched him with as neutral an expression as she could manage.

His eyes flashed with disappointment. "Go on up to bed."

She placed her hands on her hips and bolstered her courage to ask, "What about you?"

He gave her a look hot enough to melt an icicle on a subzero day. "Is that an invitation?"

She almost said yes, just barely refraining. But oh how she wanted to let him take control over what happened next. "I'll let you know in the morning."

She left him to fend for himself, wondering how she could barricade her bedroom door—or if she even wanted to. If the locks and security systems at the Institute couldn't keep him out, she doubted a chair wedged beneath the doorknob would do the trick.

No matter how much she ached to throw caution to the wind, Fallon was too level-headed to take such chances. If she'd only had herself to think about, she might have immediately said yes. But she had responsibilities to her parents, her siblings and her stockholders. She couldn't simply disappear for however long his mission lasted and have an enticing fling.

Besides, how could she trust the man with her body when she didn't believe half of his wild story? Some of the best con men in the world had tried to swindle her. She might only be twenty-eight, but she wasn't naive, and she wasn't buying his story.

If he'd known she was hallucinating, why had he asked her to drive? She could've killed them both. And why was the drug so selective, acting only when she left Kane's presence?

And his reason for breaking into her office was downright flimsy. It would take ten men five months to search through the Institute's massive computer banks to find one tiny project. How would Kane have broken the passwords?

As she walked upstairs to her bedroom, she worried over another incident that didn't fit. She'd aimed that gun at his wide chest. From less than ten feet, it was difficult to miss.

But if she'd missed, where had the bullet gone? It hadn't smashed into the television screen or splintered the wall behind him. And her white leather sofa sported no ripped fabric or furrows. She scowled at the irony of her attempt to kill the first interesting man she'd met in months, one who even cleaned up after himself in the kitchen.

Yawning, Fallon closed her bedroom door. As she walked across the airy room, decorated in soft turquoise and gold, she left a trail of clothing across the carpet. Louisa would be in tomorrow to straighten the mess.

Louisa—oh no. The maid had a key. Fallon couldn't let her walk into the house or Kane might take her prisoner, too. In the morning, she'd have to convince him that it would be convenient for him to let her make a phone call and discourage Louisa from coming to work.

After stepping into the shower, Fallon adjusted the spray and wondered what to do. She wouldn't try leaving. At this hour she wasn't up to facing the nausea again. But she did have several options—all dangerous. She could set off the panic button by her bed and silently summon the police. But could they get to her before Kane did?

Even if the police arrested Kane, what would she tell them? She'd be lucky if they didn't lock her up in a cell adjoined to his—a padded one.

However the most dangerous option of all was the one she found most enticing. Suppose she accepted his bargain? Would he come through on his promise and deliver? Would she really be able to give up control to him? And what if she said *no?* She'd already learned she couldn't stop him from taking whatever he wanted.

But the man wasn't into using force. He wanted her to willingly give herself to him to do with as he pleased—an idea she found all too appealing because then she'd have to make no further decisions. From then on, all she would need to do was succumb to his wishes, and enjoy every second.

From the heated looks he'd given her, from the electric connection between them, she had little doubt he was as aware of her as a woman as she was of him as a man. Instinct told her the lovemaking would be fantastic.

Just the thought of being so free, to give herself wholly over to another individual, caused heat to pool in her belly. After washing and rinsing her hair, she soaped the rest of her body, and her skin felt wonderfully sensitive as she imagined Kane kissing her, caressing her with those strong hands and gentle fingers. There was no denying that the idea of his touching her anywhere he pleased, however he pleased, intrigued her.

And he'd made it quite clear that once she agreed, it would be the last choice he'd allow her. She should be horrified, terrified. Instead, her breasts ached and excitement splashed through her veins.

But could she really agree to the bargain? She had no idea.

After stepping from the steamy shower, she

wrapped a towel around her, tucking the corner between her breasts. She applied moisturizer to her face, then dried her hair vigorously with another towel. Not liking to sleep with a wet head, she flipped on the blow dryer and let the warmth and the familiar motions soothe her frazzled nerves.

But somehow she didn't think she'd sleep tonight, not with him downstairs. Not with his tempting bargain preying on her mind. At least she no longer thought he'd kill her. If he was going to, he'd have done it after she'd tried to shoot him.

Instead, he'd held her a little too close before he'd handed back her gun. She could still recall his arms encompassing her, holding her tight while she tensed, waiting for the fatal shot that never came.

Had it been her imagination, or had a tremor rippled through his muscles as he held her? When she'd turned around, he'd appeared all steely and commanding. Then he'd relaxed while they sparred with words over the dinner table and a new kind of tension had started to grow.

She couldn't have missed his appreciative gaze that let her know he found her attractive. Once her fear had subsided, she'd begun to see Kane in a different light. As a man. With his dark hair, dark eyes, and a body to die for, he wore his masculinity like a shield. But it was his bargain that dominated her thoughts, twisted into her psyche and made her wonder if the drugs she'd breathed in had lowered her inhibitions. Or was it the man himself?

Whether he worked for some secret government

agency, she didn't know, but he carried himself with the bearing of a soldier, or one of those martial arts experts who moved soundlessly through the shadows. But her memories might only be hallucinations, and his seemingly impossible feats might have been simply delusions caused by the almond drug. She shook her head, fluffing the last of her hair dry and turning off the blower.

She exited the bathroom and stepped over to the dresser. Tonight she would not sleep nude. She reached for a T-shirt and shorts as if the flimsy material could protect her from him…and her own thoughts.

At the sound of an unnaturally loud click, Fallon spun around. Her towel began to slip. She gasped, her hand grabbing the terry cloth.

Kane stood beside the bed, a faint glint of humor on his lips, his eyes hungry. "I like your outfit."

FALLON POSSESSED the most incredibly sexy legs Kane had ever seen, trim ankles, sleek calves, shapely knees, and firm thighs, which the skimpy towel did little to hide. He swallowed hard, trying to remember she hadn't accepted his terms.

At the sight of him, her eyes flashed and her body went taut. "What are you doing in my room?"

"Disabling the panic button."

A bead of moisture trickled from her temple, down her creamy cheek, onto her full lip. She licked it away with the tip of her pink tongue, sending a flash of heat straight to his groin.

She padded to her closet and pulled out a robe, then donned it over the towel. "I have no intention of calling the cops."

"So you say. All the same, it's better to remove the temptation."

She straightened her spine and jerked the belt at her waist tight. For a moment, Fallon's fingers played nervously with the sash and then as if she realized what she was doing, she thrust her hands into her pockets.

Kane pulled a screwdriver from the tool chest he'd found downstairs and turned his back to her. Unfortunately, with her, out of sight was not out of mind. Damn it! He had to remember that she might not ever agree to his terms. With a determined effort, he bent to the alarm cover plate. From the corner of his eye, he watched the towel slither from beneath her robe and she kicked it away.

He gritted his teeth. Lord, the woman even had attractive feet with cute high arches and long straight toes. He imagined holding one slim foot in his hand, caressing his way up those fabulously long legs. The screwdriver thudded to the floor, and he knelt by her bed to retrieve it.

Her scent wafted up from the sheets, reminding him that while he might be eager to have her, he couldn't forget his job. Fallon was sorely testing his strength of will. It took all his self-control to kneel by the switch and place the tool on the first screw without looking in her direction.

"Don't," she said, her voice sharp.

"Why not?"

"Any attempt to tamper with the system sends a silent alarm to the police station."

"Really?"

She drew in a deep breath, and her breasts thrust against the damp material. "Why would I lie?"

"Why wouldn't you?" Kane countered, peering at her through narrowed eyes. Perhaps she intended to accept his bargain and his hopes rose. Did she have any idea how attractive she looked with her face flushed, her curls framing her high cheekbones?

"As fast as you move, you could get to me before the police did." A suggestion of awareness flickered in her eyes and then she hid it behind a facade of studied calm.

He raised his brow, wondering how hard she was fighting with herself. Lucky for him, the woman had absolutely no idea what he intended to do to her. As he imagined the courage it would take for her to give herself over to him, all the blood in his body headed below his waist.

He had to stop thinking of her as anything beyond a sex object. Now. This was not his time to let emotions cloud his judgment. Getting closer to Fallon Hanover any way but physically could only lead to disaster.

"And if the cops took you away, I'd get sick again. So exactly what is the protocol to tell one's kidnapper to get the hell out of one's bedroom?"

He glanced with regret at the panic button, unwilling to trust her. But to tamper with the backup battery or disconnect the wiring could summon the police. The technology was well within the capabilities of the early twenty-first century. However, too much rode on the outcome of this mission to leave her alone where she could easily call for help. The last thing he needed was the authorities on his tail. Maintaining a low profile had to be his first priority.

He kept his tone casual. "You don't want me to go."

"Your mind-reading abilities are way off."

"You want me. You want to accept my offer. Just the idea of being at my complete mercy is arousing to you. It's only a matter of time before you yield."

She shook her head, but she couldn't seem to summon the words to disagree. Good. He pushed her further. "You'll have to sleep downstairs with me."

As she tensed to speak, he watched the protest rise to her lips and die. Without saying another word she spun on her heel and removed some clothing from her bureau. After striding back into the bathroom, she slammed the door. A few minutes later she reappeared dressed in jeans and a well-worn T-shirt.

He followed her out of the bedroom suddenly curious about her, about the men in her life. Her too-brief dossier only contained information pertaining to her worldwide financial empire with few clues to her past, except her CIA connection—which she had yet to admit to.

One last glance over his shoulder into the bedroom didn't reveal too many hints. The only photograph in the room—a younger Fallon with an older couple, most likely her parents, standing on the bow of a yacht—didn't tell him anything about the adult woman. Those facts he'd have to discover for himself.

It couldn't hurt to find out more about her, especially if they had to spend the next several weeks together. He observed the cute way her hips sashayed as she walked in front of him. She stopped short in the hallway and removed a pillow, sheets and a blanket from a linen closet.

Kane was all too aware of the sparks she kindled in him. He knew too well that while he could enjoy sex on the job, he enjoyed it so much more when the woman fascinated him. And Fallon was one fascinating lady. He couldn't wait to explore her combination of courage and desire. He couldn't risk becoming emotionally involved, yet he knew he was smarter than he once was. In his line of work, love wasn't just a luxury—it could get him killed.

Nigel was an especially cunning thief. Underestimating his quarry would be a mistake.

When they arrived on the ground floor, she interrupted his thoughts. "Where am I supposed to sleep?" she asked in a businesslike tone, but her subterfuge didn't fool him. She didn't like the idea of sleeping near him.

"The couch."

Without looking in his direction, she floated the linen over the plush leather, tucked in the edges, and plumped the pillow. Once she'd lain down, she closed her eyes, and immediately proceeded to toss and turn. Sleeping in those tight jeans couldn't be comfortable. And that's when he realized that she wanted him to take command. She'd given him every sign of wanting him—except a verbal one.

If she couldn't make the decision to accept what she so obviously wanted, he would make it for her. He might be wrong, but he didn't think so and decided to test her. If she obeyed, he'd take that as a sign that she'd agreed to their bargain.

"You can't sleep in those clothes. Go change."

"I'm fine."

"All that tossing and turning is distracting me. And if I'm going to be distracted, it might as well be for a good cause." He gentled his tone, but kept the ring of command. "Go change into that lace night-gown that's hanging on the back of your door."

"I haven't agreed."

She hadn't said no, either. He'd taken a chance by snapping out the demand, knowing if she obeyed that she'd eventfully give him what he would ask for. "Do it. I want you to wear something sexy."

Eyes full of fire, she stood and flung off the covers. And they locked gazes. He held his breath, wondering if she could find it within her to give up control. This moment wasn't about her clothing, it was about whether she would follow his order.

Her eyes flashed with hesitation. And outrage. And interest.

He could see her fighting herself as she trembled. The air around them snapped with electricity. He waited, hoping she'd give in to what they both wanted.

And finally, head high, she headed up the stairs. He waited until she was partway up before speaking. "Fallon." She halted on the stairs and glanced over her shoulder at him and he could have sworn desire rippled through her. "Don't wear anything underneath it."

FALLON WONDERED if she'd lost her mind. Because she was going to do exactly as he asked. And while earlier, she'd thought to cooperate with the hopes of possibly intercepting some of his technical data for her country, she didn't kid herself now. She wanted to do as Kane asked for the sheer pleasure of doing so. Just thinking about wearing her long, lace gown for him caused her mouth to go dry and her belly to pull with anticipation. While Fallon had never done anything like this before, if the idea of wearing that gown for him aroused her, she couldn't imagine how much more exciting she'd find the actual act itself.

When she couldn't bring herself to agree to his bargain, he'd taken the choice from her. She supposed if she wanted to be ill again, she could attempt to leave him, however, she'd much rather don the lace gown and see where her actions led.

So once she reached her room, she shucked her jeans and T-shirt and only hesitated at her panties and bra before those items joined the rest. And after she shimmied into the five thousand dollar Chanel nightgown, she figured it was worth every penny. Standing in front of her mirror, she fluffed her hair and grinned in satisfaction. The gown revealed streaks and slashes of bare skin but still covered all the essentials. And she looked damn good in it. She watched her diet, exercised regularly, cross training between cycling, running and swimming. Still, she took a deep fortifying breath before heading back downstairs.

She knew so little about Kane. But her lack of knowledge made what she was doing all the more thrilling. Especially since she found him so attractive. And for once, she was going to forget her responsibilities and throw caution aside—even forget she could still hit the panic button. Because the idea of being totally at his mercy excited her more than any danger she'd ever placed herself in as an agent.

Chin high, she walked down the stairs, the lack of undergarments allowing her body freedom. Her breasts swaying against the lace felt decadent and decidedly perky as she anticipated Kane's reaction.

Kane leaned back in the couch, his attention on the television, but apparently sensing her presence on the stairs, he looked up and caught her gaze. His bold stare raked her, and at her sudden hesitancy, his lips curled in cool amusement. Her flesh tingled with pleasant awareness, encouraging her progress. Seeing the satisfaction glimmer in his eyes that she'd done exactly as he asked caused her pulse to accelerate. He didn't even pretend to divert his attention back to the television. As she advanced, each step toward him becoming more difficult, she realized that she'd agreed to their bargain in every way but words.

"Come." As if sensing her second thoughts, he

held out his hand and gestured for her to join him. Determined to go through with whatever he requested, she placed one foot in front of the other and crossed the last few steps. He remained seated and opened his hand. In his palm was a shiny disk about the size of a dime. "This is part of the new technology I was telling you about."

"What is it?"

"A body buff." He held it out to her.

She picked up the innocent-looking disk by the edge between thumb and pointer finger. "What does it do?"

"It's a multipurpose invention. Right now its primary purpose is to groom you."

"Excuse me?"

"Once you place it flat on your skin, the program takes over. It can't hurt you, and it won't do anything you don't want it to do."

"My thoughts control it?"

"Not exactly. Mine do." He shot her a challenging grin. "I programmed it to groom you the way I prefer. However, you can always override my decision if you don't like what the body buff is doing."

"I don't know…"

"You must learn that I understand what you want and will give that to you." He plucked the body buff from her fingers and placed it flat on her palm.

Curious but uncertain about what the gadget would do, she didn't protest. The disk in her palm tingled pleasantly and of its own accord slid up to her neck—where it divided in half, then scooted back to her fingers. She held up her hands and watched as the disks each cleaned, buffed and polished the nails of one hand with a plum-colored polish that dried upon contact.

"Amazing." She admired the buff's handiwork as it moved back up her arms and onto her face. She turned to watch her transformation in the mirror about the hearth. The body buff applied glitter over her cheeks, applied gloss on her lips and smudged eyeliner in a perfect line by her lashes. Automatically she closed her eyes and felt the featherlight touch of the disk over her lids while the other disk brushed blush on her cheeks. When it finished, she opened both eyes and stared at her reflection. It had applied a plum mascara and a soft sea-green eyeshadow. Never had she looked quite so exotic. Although she'd been made up by some of the best cosmetologists in the world, this coloring suited her skin exactly.

"Wow."

She wasn't quite done admiring the nifty device when the buffs promptly plunged below her neckline where she couldn't see them. Immediately, the dual disks began to circle her breasts. Beginning at the outermost edges, the devices made a circuit over her skin, each circuit spiraling closer toward her nipples.

"Oh…my…God." The sensation startled her, first with a wonderful warming, then a vibrating tingle. "What—"

"Relax. You're enjoying the sensation or the buff would stop. It's programmed to read your body's signals."

The prickling in her breasts was wonderful. Terrible. Arousing. And as the buffs glided over her skin, she felt them applying oil that seemed to make her flesh even more sensitive. "But what is it doing to me?"

"You may lower the gown to look if you like." He laced his hands behind his head. And then he waited to see if she would reveal her breasts—but she wasn't comfortable enough to stand in front of him and bare herself.

And then the disks found her nipples, and she almost jumped out of her skin. "Ah…it's cold…now it's hot." She gasped as pleasure shot right to her core. Kane was staring at her breasts, her nipples now budding hard with arousal right through the lace material. Without thinking, she began to raise her hands to cover her reaction.

"Do not hide your pleasure from me." His tone was not a request, not quite a demand.

She dropped her hands to her sides and wondered exactly when she'd lost the desire to do anything except what he commanded. Obeying his wishes made her realize how quickly he was conditioning her to submit to his orders. What she hadn't understood was how much she would like it. She adored his attention on her, loved the way her body was heating up. One by one he was taking away her choices, liberating her so she had nothing to do but enjoy. He was directing the body buffs for her pleasure and it…was…*good.*

Not having a choice was setting her free to enjoy

the sensations. Her breasts had never felt so tender, so achy, so feminine. But even better than the physical sensation was the idea of being so totally at his mercy.

"You like the body buffs on your breasts, don't you?"

"Yes."

"And do you know why it's called a body buff, not a breast buff?"

"Because it buffs the entire body." As soon as he led her thoughts to other possibilities, the body buffs dropped from her breasts to her stomach and skipped right down to her mons. And just like her breasts, they outlined the perimeter of the area.

But the vibration was very different. Her skin was... "Oh...my...are they shaving me?"

"Most of you."

Kane's eyes locked on hers and the intimate look combined with the knowledge of what his devices were doing made her legs weak. And yet, the sensations were indescribably delicious, tickling, gentle, softly mesmerizing. And since she liked it, they kept right on doing what they were doing.

Kane's eyes twinkled. "Want to look?"

Yes. "No." Because that would mean he would look, too. And the idea of standing before him while his device performed such intimate tasks on her caused heat to flush her face.

"Spread your legs wider so the buff can do a proper job."

She complied and her voice rose in surprise.

"It's…sliding right…oh…oh." One of the buffs had slid into the crease of her butt and was slowly going up and down and driving her insane. The other was sensuously gliding over her lips. Then one pulsing disc settled right on her clit. And the other in the most sensitive spot between her butt cheeks.

"Where are they now?" Kane asked, his tone demanding.

"You…know."

"Tell me."

She clamped her teeth down, refusing to answer. Kane acted as though he expected her resistance. He opened his hand and held out another disc. "By now your breasts could probably use more attention."

Was he doubling the sensations because she hadn't immediately answered him? She had no idea. But she was in no condition to resist him again, nor did she want to. Instead, she took the disk, placed it on her palm and it immediately scooted up her arm, divided in half and then busily went to work on her breasts. The sensation gently excited her but just as she began to relax into the stimulation, the disks altered their pattern.

All four discs began to vibrate in tandem, the rhythms playing off one another and shooting fizzing pulses through her. Standing became more difficult. The lacy gown that was covering her skin seemed more of a hindrance than a necessity.

She wanted the gown off. She wanted Kane's clothes off. She wanted him to make love to her, to touch her where the disks had and to trace his lips over her sensitive skin.

She raised a hand to release the tie between her breasts that held up her gown. Kane shook his head. "I didn't give you permission to undress."

Damn him. Not even undressing was to be her choice. She should have been upset. Annoyed. But his taking all control had her head swimming and her body so aroused that she could barely stand. "May I undress?"

"Are you certain you want to stand in front of me naked?"

"Yes."

"For as long as I like?"

With his heated eyes on her? "Yes."

"You understand that I may or may not touch you? The decision is all mine."

"Yes." His words caused exhilarating anticipation and her nipples tightened and poked into the lace of the gown, showing him exactly how much she liked his suggestion. Doing what he wished excited her in a way she hadn't known was possible.

"Fine. Then you may take off your gown. But do it slowly. And while you disrobe, I want you to look me in the eyes. I want you to understand that you have no rights except those that I give you. You will have no pleasure except what I allow you to have."

Oh… She was shaking with need—he knew exactly how to turn her on, yet he hadn't so much as touched her or kissed her. And she was going to be standing there naked. Waiting for him. And loving every second.

5

FALLON HAD NEVER stripped for anyone before, not even for Allen during their short-lived marriage. But her feminine instincts had no difficulty taking over. She played with the ribbon that tied her bodice together. Then ever-so-slowly, she unfastened the bow. As directed, she kept her gaze on Kane, fascinated by how his dark blue eyes smoked.

She exposed the deep vee of skin between her breasts, allowing her fingers to enticingly pull back the gown's edges to reveal more skin. And while she might have been obeying his commands, the power was all hers.

His Adam's apple bobbed up and down. His cool amusement remained on his mouth, but a cord in his neck throbbed to reveal he was anticipating her next move with every cell in his body. She'd never had a man's attention focused so intensely on her and only her. It was as if they were the only two people in the world, and with every sliver of skin she exposed, the connection between them swelled, filling up the air around them until she had trouble drawing a breath.

She hooked a finger under the spaghetti strap at

her shoulder and let it fall over her bicep. She began to do the same on the other side, drawing out the moment. But then with an impish grin, she shrugged her bared shoulder and the gown's bodice fell to reveal one breast.

"Nice. Very nice." The compliment seemed tugged from his lips without his permission. As if regretting he'd said anything at all, he drew his brows together. "Stay right there for now."

Fallon barely dared to draw a breath. The gown, held up by one flimsy strap could fall at any time. Just moments ago, she would have sworn that was exactly what she'd wanted. But standing and waiting was even sexier. With one breast bared to the air, she'd never felt so wanton.

Kane gave her a knowing look and then placed television headphones over his ears. And she realized he wasn't pausing her striptease for just a few seconds; he meant to leave her like that until he decided he wanted more. Stopping her just as her courage and desires had converged into seething determination not only upset her but it tilted her equilibrium.

Annoyed, aroused and aggravated, she almost spun on her heel and fled back to her room. But he cleared his throat and shook his head in warning. He wanted her right there and as that knowledge hissed through her, moisture seeped between her thighs. Damn. She was enjoying his domination.

The realization coiled around her gut and rose up her throat to choke her. This couldn't be happening. She shouldn't be so turned on by following Kane's demands. But she was. And though the liberated woman in her wanted to deny her reaction with every atom of her being, she couldn't deny her own nature. It wasn't his command keeping her there, but her own heated reaction to his command.

And damn him, he knew. From the cool amusement in his eyes to the upward smirk of his lips, he understood exactly what was happening to her. She might not like herself very much right now for playing his games, but no way did she want to quit. Oh no. Kane and his gadgets and her own nature were exciting her to the point that she was trembling with a cauldron of emotions. But the feeling that rose to the top of the boiling pot was exhilaration. She might be trapped by her own need to give him exactly what he asked for, but she intended to enjoy every moment.

Even as Kane used the remote control, she stood still, knowing his attention would return to her shortly. And she thought about what he would ask her to do and how much she would enjoy doing it.

Meanwhile, Kane flipped the channels. "I'm starting my search for Nigel by tracking the news channels."

Apparently he could hear her through the headphones. "Why?"

"I'm listening for a news story that doesn't fit. He's going to try and sell his stolen technology and it'll probably make the news. It's my job to stop him."

From her position to one side of him, Fallon

peered through her lashes and saw that his gaze had left her to focus on the television. When she saw he had no current interest in her, she let her gaze take in all of him. He'd gone from turning her on with one burning gaze to focusing on business in less than the span of a television commercial. And yet, she had no doubt he hadn't forgotten about her. She certainly was very aware of him. His breathing patterns remained steady, but a knotted muscle by his jaw told her he wasn't as unaffected by her as he pretended.

However, when he pressed the remote control unit buttons faster than an executive secretary typed, she had to wonder what the hell he was doing. The pictures on her giant screen focused and changed so swiftly she barely formed an image before he clicked to the next. At first she expected him to stop when a program caught his eye. But he continued to flip the channels in a mystifying manner for at least ten minutes before shutting off the set.

And each minute seemed both interminable and, contradictorily, to fly by with amazing speed. In either case, she was left wondering what he would do next. One moment she wanted him to kiss her, the next she hoped he'd simply be tired of the game until she could collect herself.

She should have known he wouldn't tire easily. He rested the remote control on his knee. "You failed to keep your gaze on me."

Her mouth went dry. His tone told her there would be consequences for her failure to obey and heat flashed over her skin. She forced her gaze back to his, a gaze that shocked her with its intensity.

"Without bending, lift your gown."

She bunched her hands in the lace and slowly drew the hem up from the floor past her ankles, her calves, her knees. There was something utterly wicked about standing there and revealing herself at his command. Her heart pounded and her breasts tingled.

"Higher."

She drew the lace up to her thighs.

Fallon wanted to shut her eyes or look away, not out of humiliation or embarrassment but because she didn't want him to know how excited she was. But being unable to hide her thrill from him was yet another turn-on. The material on her thigh tickled and taunted and she eased it a smidgen higher.

"Not enough."

The cool air-conditioning was riding up under her gown. Without panties, with most of her pubic hair gone, she was about to expose herself to those burning eyes. She'd never been this vulnerable—or this ready to follow his command to the letter. He no longer bothered to hold her gaze. Oh no. He was watching her raise the hem. Watching her put herself on display.

Her stomach tightened. She couldn't believe she was having so much fun. Couldn't believe how pleasing him aroused her.

His voice turned husky, demanding. "Higher."

Hands trembling with eagerness, she lifted the

gown above her thighs. The lace hem teased her newly shaved mons, then skimmed over the slender triangle of hair that he'd allowed her to keep.

The material cleared her pubic area and fluttered across her hips leaving her feeling totally decadent and seductive. His eyes took her in and heat burst in her belly. She sucked in a breath to steady her jumpy nerves.

"Turn around. Slowly."

Oh…my. She should have expected the request. Should have realized the material wasn't just above her mons but above her bottom, too. She began to turn but not before she spied the arrogant satisfaction in his eyes. But she couldn't wait to turn around so he couldn't see her face. She was wild with the need to hide her longing and relished a moment to re-group.

Except when she turned, she hadn't counted on the mirror. All along he'd had a front and back view—but she hadn't realized that until she'd turned. And if the sight of her body displayed and posed for him made her want to squirm, the excitement on her face almost set off panic.

Just one look at her face told him how much she was enjoying complying to his commands. She should be running away. But she wouldn't, not when she had the opportunity to explore a side of herself that she hadn't known existed until tonight.

How far would he push her? She didn't know. How far would she go? She had no idea. And not knowing thrilled her, tested her, challenged her in ways that made her feel fully alive. If anyone had told her that obeying Kane's commands could arouse her, she would have laughed in their face. But she wasn't laughing now.

She was holding her breath. Waiting for him to tell her what he wanted next. Or maybe he wouldn't say anything at all. Just leave her in limbo, upping her anticipation another few degrees.

"Drop the gown to the floor."

She released the hem, sorry when she was again covered except for one bare breast. In the mirror, he must have seen the disappointment on her face. But he ignored her again, shoved to his feet and strode to her work desk and computer. He booted the system and she watched his face in the mirror, wanting to see his expression when he failed to crack her password.

But the keys clicked nonstop, his fingers a blur of motion. A secret agent typing over two hundred words a minute?

"Would you like to help with my search?"

There were other things she'd rather do. However, she could use the time to collect herself. "Sure."

"All right. Lose the gown and come here." He patted the arm of his chair, indicating where he wanted her to sit and simply assuming she would get naked for him. She'd been so ready to take it off a few minutes ago. But he'd given her time to cool down, no doubt just to heat her up again.

Annoyed with her own hesitation, her pulse racing, she shrugged out of the remaining spaghetti strap, shimmied once to free the material from her hips and stepped out of the gown. With his back to her, he didn't even watch her disrobe or approach. And yet, heart dancing up her throat, she obeyed to the letter, stepping toward his chair.

Gingerly, she sat on the arm of the chair, taking care not to brush against him. The cool leather against her bare bottom combined with her agitation caused the chair to teeter. He missed a few keystrokes and stopped typing.

"Perhaps you'd be more comfortable on my lap." He worded his statement as a suggestion but gave her no choice. His large hands closed around her waist and he lifted her off the chair's arm and set her down.

The warmth of his hands on her cool skin made her gasp. And with him sitting there fully dressed while she wore nothing made her very aware of his hard thighs under her bottom, his powerful chest against her back. Unsettled by his maneuver, she sat stiff and wary. With his breath fanning her neck, his arms reaching around her for the keyboard, he'd neatly trapped her. She was all too aware of how close his arms were to her breasts, how easily he could touch her.

Corporate names, government agencies and private telephone numbers flashed on the screen and disappeared. When he logged onto the Internet and bypassed the Pentagon's code, an icy tentacle wrapped around her gut.

"Who are you?"

"It's okay, I'm authorized." Kane spoke without

slowing his typing, seemingly unconcerned by the secrets he revealed. Obviously, Kane, or whoever he was, worked at the loftiest levels of her government to have access codes to such high-security agencies.

"What are you looking for?"

"Something out of the ordinary. Something that doesn't fit the pattern."

"What pattern?"

Kane worked his way through the daily newspapers next, the pages blinking by too fast for her to read them. She didn't expect him to explain, but Kane seemed to make a habit of doing the unexpected. "If Nigel intends to sell the stolen information, he has to find a buyer."

She couldn't believe she was sitting naked on his lap having an ordinary conversation. The discs had settled to a soothing thrumming, keeping her on edge as she wondered what he'd programmed them to do next. Thinking about his mission was almost impossible while sitting on his lap, breathing in his scent, a crisp scent that was dominating and very male.

Every breath she took caused friction between her back against his chest. The growing hardness behind her bottom told her he was very aware of her skin next to his. However, she forced herself to focus. "But you don't know exactly what Nigel took, so how can you guess who the buyer might be?"

"To optimize his sale and find the highest bidder, he only has limited choices of the wealthiest of—"

She frowned at the screen. "Hey. That's illegal. You're reading private e-mail." Fallon recognized the names of America's leaders in banking, insurance and finance.

"Spread your legs."

She'd been sitting with her knees pressed together, her ankles crossed. His sudden demand had her heart skipping. Unlocking her ankles, she allowed her knees to part a few inches.

"Wider."

Oh…my…ah. She bit her bottom lip to keep from releasing a soft moan as she draped her legs over his and her bottom snuggled deeper against him.

"Now lean your head back against me."

She did as she asked, realizing that the motion lifted her breasts. He took her hands that had been on her thighs and placed them to either side of the chair. She was squirming inside and the kindling desire burst into licking flames. He'd draped her over him and her parted legs released her musky scent into the air, telling him quite clearly that she was moist and needy and eager for whatever he wanted to do next.

Kane continued scanning the correspondence of some of the country's biggest financial institutions. And she sat still, her legs parted and open, wondering if he was ever going to touch her. Her nipples were so tight, the ache between her thighs so intense that sitting still was sweet torture. But even worse, her breath was beginning to sound raspy. Hiding her arousal was no longer an option. She needed him to touch her. His hands were so close, but he had only made physical contact with her once to lift her to position her on his lap. She wanted to beg him to stroke her.

She was trembling with her need, wondering if it was possible to find release by mental stimulation alone. Damn it. With her legs parted and draped over his, her mons shaved, he should be eager to touch her. But he didn't, and every second seemed like…forever.

"Nigel's dangerous. He can sell to the government, private industry or—yes. I think I've found him. He's going to attempt to sell a stolen item at Kendals, an auction house."

Good. Perhaps now he'd turn off the computer and pay some much-desired attention to her plump lips that had never felt so engorged. Surely he hadn't asked her to undress, sit on him and open her legs so he could ignore her.

"Does Kendals ever sell technology?"

At his question, she wanted to sob in frustration. "Don't you want to touch me?"

"I will do what I wish with you when I wish it. I thought I'd made that clear."

"But—"

"You will not tell me what you want. I will give you what you need. Understood?"

She couldn't believe he would deny her. She tried to squeeze her legs together to attain a measure of relief. But his thighs stopped her, holding her legs open.

"Do you understand?" he repeated.

"Yes," she hissed, understanding all too well.

She'd thought she couldn't possibly become more aroused. But as he refused to touch her, tiny jolts of electricity seemed to ratchet her to another level.

"Does Kendals ever auction off technology?" he repeated his question.

She could barely concentrate on his words. Kendals was an auction house that specialized in fine art. "They usually sell rare art, jewelry, antiques. Collectors' items."

"Then this is it. We'll leave for New York immediately."

Fallon's head was spinning. She was on edge, her nerves raw and her mind clouded with need. She was barely able to recall that she had three important meetings scheduled for tomorrow, one with the Chinese ambassador. And she couldn't miss giving the Chamber speech she'd promised for their annual woman's luncheon.

"I have a business to run. I can't go gallivanting across the country."

Before he could answer, car headlights struck the blinds and washed the room with a glaring brilliance. In one graceful motion, Kane flipped off the computer, backed the chair from the desk and rolled them to the floor.

"Stay down."

She landed on her bottom before he flattened her with his body. His chest pressed against hers and his hand covered her mouth. She struggled for a moment against his weight until she realized the futility of escape. No way could she dislodge him.

Kane's eyes glistened in the glaring light. "Don't make a sound," he whispered, waiting for her to nod her compliance before removing his hand from her mouth.

Someone pounded on the front door, rang the bell, then resumed pounding. "Fallon. Yoo-hoo! Fallon, honey. I know you're inside!"

"It's Sinclair. He's family," she whispered, ignoring Kane's instructions to remain silent since Sinclair would never hear her above the knocking. She'd recognize her stepbrother's whining voice anywhere, even without his periodic nocturnal visits. Sinclair's last attempt to run one of the Hanover subsidiaries five years ago had been a disaster. Since then his occasional binge drinking had declined into a state of steady alcoholism. From the sound of him, he was on a good bender, although at the silly, not yet obnoxious stage.

Fallon shoved against Kane's shoulder. "Let me up."

Kane didn't budge, but watched her with smoldering intensity. "Who's Sinclair?" He caught her chin, and brushed his thumb lightly over her mouth in a slow, fiercely intimate gesture, causing a shiver of pleasure to race through her.

She refused to think about how exciting she found Kane's touch. She refused to think how much she wanted to rip off his clothes. Instead, she had to dress and deal with the problem. "Sinclair is my stepbrother. He believes in treating all women as sequels so his latest wife divorced him. He shows up here occasionally."

"In the middle of the night?"

Kane rolled off her, muscles rippling across his shoulder blades. He held out his hand and helped her to her feet, the contact of his palm sending a wave of sensation through her.

Get a grip. She stood straight, but it still wasn't enough to bring the top of her head any higher than his shoulder. She bent and reached for her gown to dress, wishing she had a thick robe to cover herself.

"I didn't tell you to dress."

She pulled the gown over her head and let it flutter to her feet. "No way am I dealing with him naked."

Kane placed his hands on her shoulders and spun her to look in the mirror. "This is what he'll see."

Fallon gasped. In the mirror, she appeared to be fully dressed in slacks, a blouse and jacket. But when she looked down at herself, she was still clad in the lace gown. "How?"

"Oh my darling sister Fallon. Oh my darrrrling Fal-al-lon. You can't be lost and gone forever…"

Fallon groaned.

Kane kept his voice low. "I can't explain the buff's technology. Suffice it to say, that drunk isn't going to see one inch of you that he shouldn't."

And she couldn't help noting his possessive tone. She didn't understand how the device worked, and for a moment she thought of the story of "The Emperor's New Clothes," in which he walks around and everyone pretends he's really clad in silver- and gold-threaded garments. But another look in the mirror reassured her that Kane was telling her the truth.

Time to deal with Sinclair. "He'll stand out there and bellow all night if I don't talk to him." When Kane still seemed undecided, she added, "The neighbors might hear."

"What's he want?"

"Money would be my first guess."

Finally, Kane nodded. "All right. But get rid of him quick."

While Kane remained in the living room, Fallon hurried to the front door and opened it, half-expecting Sinclair to ogle her in the nightgown. Instead, he almost fell on top of her.

Sinclair's breath reeked of rum. She noted the top three buttons of his custom-tailored shirt were missing. As he staggered toward her, she straight-armed him in a defensive gesture, shoving him to one side.

Unsteady after her thrust, he stumbled backward against the door, effectively shutting it before he collapsed in a heap. Sprawled on the hard granite with his feet stretched out in front of him, he hiccupped. "S'excuse me."

His boyish looks and shadowed pain no longer swayed Fallon to see his side. Sinclair needed to grow up. She took in his glazed pupils and bloodshot eyes. "How much did you lose?"

His dignity lost several drinks ago, he crawled across the floor and wrapped his arms around her ankles. "I wor—sip, worship at your feet."

"Right. You worship the ground my grandfather struck oil on. What are you going to cost me this time?"

He sent her his most charming, albeit lopsided, grin. "You still love your little brother, don't you?"

"I don't have time for this. How much?"

Kane strode forward, clearly not worried that Sinclair would see him. Besides, she doubted Sinclair would remember a thing tomorrow morning. Her stepbrother glanced at Kane but didn't acknowledge the man. Many women found Sinclair sweet and endearing. Fallon knew better. He wasn't sensitive but weak. His latest ex, Margaret, had grown tired of being a full-time lover, playmate and mother to him. Once she'd discovered that Sinclair's constant demand for attention hid a deep insecurity, she'd filed for divorce.

"Fallon, I loved Margaret at first sight."

"You saw her first in her Rolls."

"You're a hard woman, my love. But I'll pay you back, this time. I swear." He crossed his fingers over his heart. "I need five."

Kane plucked her purse off the bench and shoved it into her hands. "Just pay him the five hundred so he'll leave." He sounded irritated that she hadn't yet managed to get rid of Sinclair.

Sinclair might be drunk but he was shrewd and street smart. From the sly angle of his head, she guessed that he sensed opportunity in Kane's impatience. "But five hundred's not enough to keep me in rum for a week. I had a run of bad luck at the tables."

"If you didn't have bad luck, you wouldn't have any luck at all." She took her checkbook from her purse. "Will five grand cover you?"

Sinclair hiccupped. "Five. Hundred. Thousand. Or they'll kill me."

At the astronomical debt, she rolled her eyes to the ceiling and reined in her temper. Fallon preferred to give the money to research a cure for cancer than to waste it on her stepbrother's debts. "You gambled away half a million dollars?"

Kane handed her a pen. "Pay him."

"I lost my lucky rabbit's foot," Sinclair whined.

"That's a poor substitute for horse sense."

Each time Fallon responded to her stepbrother, Kane's scowl deepened. "Give him what he wants so he will leave."

Fallon didn't like Kane's attitude. Why must every man insist on telling her how to spend her money? Perhaps she was overly sensitive, but she'd been burned too many times to think otherwise. Wealth made a difference in how men looked at women. And the superrich didn't lead normal lives. Just once she'd like to meet someone who wanted just her, Fallon. Not Fallon Hanover, the heiress. Pleased she didn't even have to lie, she'd thwart them both. "I don't keep that much cash in my checking account."

Luckily she'd never told Sinclair about the basement and what she kept down there. Her rainy day room. If her stepbrother had had any idea what she'd stored away for emergencies in the safe, he would have spent it long ago. Sinclair had once pawned her priceless Picasso for a measly ten thousand dollars, for Pete's sake.

But she couldn't help feeling sorry for him. And so she'd given him handouts over the years. But five hundred grand was ridiculous. The payouts had to stop.

Kane ambled over to the computer. Keys clicked in a steady stream. "Sinclair, your real name is Warren Sinclair Christopher III?"

"Hey." Sinclair's eyes brightened. "How d'you know that?"

"And you bank at Morgan Guarantee and Trust?"

"So? What of it?"

"I just transferred Fallon's funds into your account," Kane said as casually as if he'd just borrowed a dollar from her purse. His voice softened dangerously. "Now get out before I change my mind."

How dare he break into her account and give away her money? While she wouldn't notice the difference, that wasn't the point. She might be willing to accept his dominance in the bedroom, but her life beyond that was another matter. She reined in her anger to speak in a civilized tone of voice. "You're awfully free with my money."

Kane shrugged. "You'll never miss it."

"So true." Sinclair shook Kane's hand. "Nebber happen again."

She ground her teeth together. "This is absolutely the last time I bail you out."

Sinclair shuffled to the front door. "You let him control your accounts? How come you never trusted—"

"Sinclair, the car keys," she demanded, unwilling to have his death on her conscience. "Call a cab on your cell. You're in no condition to drive."

Sinclair fumbled, tossing her his keys. "You do have some feelings for me, darling."

"Enough to let you wait for your ride on the front curb. I'll have your car sent over tomorrow."

After Sinclair left, Fallon sank onto the couch. She combed her fingers through her hair, wondering what Kane must think of her family.

She sighed and hugged a pillow to her chest. Less than an hour ago, she couldn't have imagined having a conversation with Kane. Her mind had been focused on sex. And although she wondered why she cared what Kane thought, she tried to explain her overprotectiveness of her stepbrother. "Sinclair wasn't always like that."

Kane took a seat across from her. "Are you referring to his gambling, his drinking or his greed?"

She tossed the pillow at his face and he dodged easily. "Never mind. I must be really tired to be talking to you. Men are damn expensive. Over the years, bailing out my stepbrother from one failed business after another, never mind his affairs and failed marriages, has cost me plenty." Her own failed marriage had cost her more.

"But it's not the money you object to losing, is it?"

Kane's perceptiveness surprised her. She hadn't thought him capable of seeing through the careful veneer with which she faced the world. But she wouldn't admit that he was right. When she'd been younger, she'd tried to help Sinclair by giving him money and advice, but she'd quickly learned that Sinclair found her help demeaning. As had Allen, her ex-husband.

Fallon stared past Kane's right shoulder, unable to meet his gaze. "Money is what I used to swap for what I thought would make me happy."

Kane leaned forward. "You still have no idea what makes you happy, do you?"

6

FALLON RAN HER HAND through her short curls. "I no longer require some man to make my day."

"Sounds lonely."

"Sometimes it is," she admitted. "I do have friends. But I'd rather be alone than live with a man I don't like." She stared straight into Kane's eyes and their gazes tuned in to one another. "What about you? Are you married?"

"No."

"In love?"

Kane stood and paced in front of the fireplace with his hands clasped behind his back, his body as tense as she'd ever seen it, telling her that something had gone very wrong in his life. "In my line of work, there's little time for love."

She raised herself on her elbow to look at him and thought of the moment he'd tackled her. He'd covered her body with his own to protect her, yet hadn't crushed her with his full weight. As her gaze wandered over his broad shoulders and flat stomach, she recalled the hard feel of him against her, his masculine smell mixed with the scent of almonds. And all that had come after. His dominance. Her arousal. He was certainly a man who knew his way around a woman. He'd proven that to her today—more times than she could count. Without her saying a word, he'd known exactly how to excite her, tempt her and keep her right on the edge of desire. But he'd also known how to care. When she'd been ill, he'd handed her a cool, damp towel to put on her neck. And after she'd tried to shoot him, he'd given her back the gun. He might pretend to be hard core, but there was a compassionate side of him that made her believe there was a woman he'd cared about in his past.

"Surely you've been in love," she mused.

He didn't so much as stiffen, but pain shadowed his eyes. "She's dead."

So her guess had been on target. "I didn't mean to rake up painful memories. I'm sorry."

"There's no need. She lived a very happy life. Ninety-three years to be exact. She had four children, twelve grandchildren and twenty-seven great-grandchildren."

Fallon had no idea what to say to that and was back to thinking she'd hooked up with a crazy man. Only he wasn't insane. He had a shrewd mind, a keen intelligence and an emotional maturity that beckoned to her. She remembered the strange things he did, the silent ease with which he moved across a room, his expertise when he'd broken into her computer, the odd way he "watched" television and body-buff gadgets so sophisticated she had no idea what kind of technology powered them.

Perhaps she hadn't heard him correctly. His words didn't make sense. Kane looked about thirty; even if he was ten years older, his numbers made no sense. Yet, why would he lie? Even she couldn't mistake the sorrow jammed tight in his voice or miss the open longing in his tone.

The silence deepened, and Kane paced like a caged lion. But his measured steps lulled her, and she rested her head on her pillow. After the long day, first her fright, then the emotional upheavals and finally dealing with Sinclair, she was worn-out. As the moon sank in the Floridian sky, Fallon's eyes closed and she fell asleep.

WHEN SHE OPENED her eyes, refreshed after a good night's sleep, she thought she was the crazy one. The sounds of heavy traffic, horns, trucks and sirens awakened her. Silken sheets caressed her skin and the scent of fresh orchids made her think of summer.

The night was long gone and daylight shone brightly. She was lying in a bed in what looked like a well-appointed hotel room with a high ceiling, papered in rich maroon and gray. Looking past a pigeon on the window, she noted an expanse of blue sky and one little puff of white cloud, like a ship lost and alone upon the sea.

She raced to the window. The sun winked a mocking good morning on a myriad of glass windows and asphalt pavement. And outside, Fallon beheld the elegant skyscrapers of New York City. She had no memory of leaving her home in Florida, no memory of the journey. The last thing she remembered was dozing on her living room couch. Either Kane had drugged her, or he'd whisked her here the same way he'd done when he'd taken her from her office to the ground floor of her building. His mode of transport might be disconcerting, but it was way better than traveling—even in her private jet. Yet, she would have been happier if he'd let her in on his plans.

And where was he? Still wearing her lace gown, she opened the door to reveal that he'd reserved an entire suite. While she was certain he was again spending her money, she appreciated waking alone so she could get her bearings. A hotel brochure clued her in to her location. Hotel Nuance was located a block from Times Square.

Before she took her shower, she realized she should order clothes to be delivered from one of their exclusive shops. But there was no phone by her bed—just an empty jack, letting her know that Kane still didn't trust her.

And why should he? She had yet to make up her own mind whether to help him or try to stop him from completing his mission. She needed more information before she could decide, and so far, he'd been mighty stingy with data. In fact, the technology had given her more clues than he had. Her problem was that as many times as she added up the clues, she could only come to one utterly impossible conclusion.

His technology was simply so superior to anything she'd ever seen that she was down to two equally unbelievable theories. Either Kane was an alien who came from another world…or he came from the future.

She entered the marble and mirrored bathroom, used the toilet, then turned on the shower and slid out of her nightgown. When she caught sight of herself in the mirror, she gasped. She had golden tattoos on her breasts, mons and buttocks and she recalled how Kane had told her that the body buff would groom her daily to match his desires. He must have programmed it to do the job on a daily basis. The sparkling swirls emphasized her erogenous zones so blatantly that heat rose up her neck.

Oh…my. Did Kane ever have an imagination. In the tiny strip of hair was embedded what appeared to be a diamond encrusted ring. And when she looked more closely, there were rings that appeared glued to her breasts. Three rings on each nipple. Tingling between her legs suggested another on her clit and several between the cheeks of her bottom.

She stepped into the shower but the cool water didn't sluice away the decorations any more than it sluiced away her sudden excitement. Kane might have come to New York to find Nigel, but he was keeping his side of the bargain.

"Good morning." Kane zapped into the bathroom. Elegant and relaxed, he picked up her gown and took a seat on the counter as if he had every right to watch her.

"Haven't you heard of knocking?"

He chuckled, eyeing her appreciatively. "Where would be the surprise in that?"

She sighed and dabbed shampoo into her unsteady hand. Hell, he'd already seen her naked; his stare shouldn't be any big deal. It was more his arrogant belief that he had every right to be here that she found disconcerting. The knowledge that he could do whatever he wanted, look for however long he wanted, already had her on edge.

"Are these marks on my body permanent?"

"They will last until tomorrow when I'll reprogram the body buff to groom you again."

So she would wake up every day with her flesh marked by him. The notion should have offended her. It didn't. She allowed the soothing citrus scent of the shampoo to calm her, then rinsed. Shaving wasn't necessary. With the exception of the hair on her head and her mons, the rest of her was as smooth and hairless as a baby's belly thanks to the body buff that had worked while she slept.

"Showering isn't really necessary. The buff keeps you clean." He held out soap to her. "However, I'll enjoy watching you wash your body."

She'd bet he would. She bit back a grin. If he wanted a show, she was going to give him one that she hoped would lead to some lusty lovemaking on the king-size bed, or chair, or right here in the shower. With no phones, she had no way to let anyone know where she was and felt as though she were playing hooky. She might as well enjoy herself…and him.

Dressed in black slacks and a white shirt, yet barefoot, Kane was a mix of formal and casual. She imagined that he'd come to her before he'd finished dressing and she liked the idea that he'd wanted to see her so badly that he hadn't stopped to don his shoes. She liked even better the notion of turning him on so they could make love. So she held the soap under the water and built up a good lather.

She began by smoothing the soap over her neck and arms, careful to turn so the spray let the suds drizzle over her chest and back. The heat in Kane's eyes was all the response she required. Oh, yeah. He liked watching her. And she liked him watching her.

The sensual connection between them simmered, but the emotional connection was ready to boil over. Raising her gown to expose herself to him, then sitting on his lap naked had caused her to get over her inhibitions with amazing speed. Now she wanted what he'd promised and couldn't think of a better way to start the day than to take off his clothes, run her hands over his flesh and taste his mouth.

Showering in front of him would be her way to make him come undone. He looked entirely too in command and she couldn't wait to put a dent in his armor.

But then with a gruff command, he interrupted her fantasy. "Face me and take the nipple rings between your soapy fingers."

Her breath hitched at his demand. She should have known those rings that attached to her were not pure decoration. Uncertain how tender her skin would be, she put down the soap and gingerly touched the third ring on her breast, the largest ring but the one farthest from her nipple. Her skin tingled but before she could do more than touch, he stopped her exploration.

"Those aren't the nipple rings."

She moved her fingers to the tiny ring on the end of her nipples. When she held the ring, she learned that they weren't three separate loops but spiraled into one another. And sensation rippled not just across the very tips but across her areolae.

Startled by the exquisite stirring ache, she jerked up her gaze to find his searing gaze boring into hers. "Pluck the rings and release them."

She did as he asked and a thrill of excitement shot through her. She released a breathy sigh. "This is going to be fun."

"So you like that?"

"Yes."

"Do it again."

She pulled at the rings and released them and wondered if she'd grown a bit more sensitive. The zing had increased. Her stomach was twisting into a knot of desire and although she told her body to slow down, it wasn't listening.

"Again," he demanded.

And she obeyed without hesitation, welcoming the wash of pleasure and blissful wonder. She wanted to pluck her nipples again and squirmed a little that he was going to decide when and if she could do so.

"You want to do that again, don't you?"

"Yes."

"Continue washing your body. But don't touch any of the rings."

Disappointment and anticipation collided. But she picked up the soap, so very aware that her plan to tease him had backfired. He was sitting comfortably on the counter, while she…she was coming unglued. She wanted to touch her breasts so badly that she had to bite her lower lip to keep from asking his permission to do so.

And as her hands soaped the rest of her, she realized how easily she'd yielded control to him. She had no idea what he'd do next. What he'd ask her to do next. She hoped they would end up making love but was content to wait and let the tension build, especially when she found the unknown so completely thrilling.

She had nothing to do but think about pleasure and that in and of itself was exciting. Fallon couldn't remember a time when she had concentrated so fully on herself. It was depraved and degenerate and erotic and exotic and she adored every second of wondering what he'd tell her to do next.

"Rinse."

She rinsed quickly and shut off the water. She stepped out of the shower and reached for a towel.

He plucked it from the rack a moment before her fingers reached for it. "I'll dry you."

"Okay." Finally. Her wait for him to touch her was almost over.

"But first, we need to finish hooking you up."

"Hooking me up?"

She stood on a bath rug, soaking wet under the bright fluorescent light. Her skin glowed with the gold sparkling tattoos and the rings attached to her skin. He flicked on a warming light and walked around her once, then stopped in front of her and raised his hand. He opened his fist and she saw a ball of fine gold links.

"I'm attaching this chain to your rings."

She sucked in her breath. He held a lot of chain in his hand but it was the deviltry in his eyes that clued her in that they wouldn't be making love anytime soon.

"Hold still."

He raised her hand toward her breast and her nipple hardened before he so much as touched her. But he didn't even graze her flesh. The chain seemed to attach itself to the center ring by some kind of magnetic attraction. Then he let out the chain as if releasing a thread from a spool and the chain attached to the ring on her other nipple. With every rise and fall of her chest, the chain tugged her nipples.

And he still had lots of chain left in his hands and a bright merriment in his dark blue eyes. Within moments he'd formed the chain into a *T,* with the ends attached to her nipples and a long section dangled unattached between her legs.

She hadn't thought this through. She'd known about the other rings but had forgotten about them during her shower. He was going to chain her erogenous zones together and she had no idea what to expect after that.

"Spread your legs." He ordered. And then he knelt and waited for her to obey.

Her mouth went dry, her stomach tightened. But she opened her legs and again he attached the chain without touching her. He connected the chain to the ring in her pubic hair, then guided it downward until the ring on her clit was also linked. Just breathing shot the most lovely tension through her, tugging the hair, shooting teeny shocks to her clit and nipples.

And he wasn't done.

"Turn around. Place your hands on the counter."

She did as he asked, desperate for the support of the marble. She didn't think too much about his view of her bare bottom and parted legs. How could she when each movement jiggled, teased and taunted her nerve endings?

She licked her bottom lip. "How long am I… when will you take off…"

He didn't answer. She already knew that he would keep her in the exquisite chain until *he* decided it was time to release her. And she suspected nothing she said would alter her situation. She would enjoy the caresses until he decided otherwise.

"Bend over. And spread your legs wider. I need to make sure every ring is attached precisely where it will do the most good."

The most good?

Oh…she…could barely hold still. The cool chain on her hot flesh made her feel wicked and vulnerable. Talk about yanking her chain. She couldn't wait for him to do so.

He knelt again and she closed her eyes as she imagined him looking at her bottom and between her now practically hairless legs. As if he were bent on making her squirm even more, he demanded, "Look at yourself in the mirror. And think about how you are letting me chain you because you want me to."

She forced her eyes open, wondering how he'd known that she'd closed them. He was between her legs, seeing everything, attaching the chain to… "Ah…oh…not…there," she whispered.

"Tell me you want this chain."

She hesitated and he tugged the chain. Pure sensation arched across her most sensitive places. And so help her, she did want this.

"Say it."

"I want the chain."

"For how long?" He was testing her.

"For as long as you want me to wear it."

He laughed and drew the chain between her legs, up between her buttocks, the contact points of her sensitive flesh already sizzling. The chain split and formed a vee over her hips and he hooked it back around the front to her nipples.

He straightened as she looked in the mirror. Her eyes were too big, her mouth lush and wanton. She looked as if she'd just tumbled out of bed all satisfied. Only she'd had no satisfaction. The damn man had yet to touch her. But his every breath kindled embers and jangled and reverberated through her. She could think of nothing but her breasts aching for his touch, of the ring that tugged her clit and sparked her desire.

"I will dry you now."

She began to straighten and stand.

He swatted her bottom. "I didn't tell you to move." The sting of his palm was nothing compared to the tug of the chain on the rings. It was if he'd plucked them all at once and the electric tension elicited a soft moan from the back of her throat. She'd never felt anything so absolutely delicious in her life.

She wanted him to swat her again. Instead he took the towel and began to dry her. Never once did he let his hand touch her flesh, careful to keep the thick terry between them. But every single smoothing of her flesh jarred the chains and she shivered uncontrollably.

She told herself that when she stood, the chain would go slack and the sensations wouldn't be so stimulating. However, as he dried her bottom and between her legs, she raised up her toes and arched her spine. When she realized what she was doing, she groaned.

If she didn't get a grip, he'd soon have her begging. Just as she was beginning to think that she'd allowed him too much control over her, he rubbed the towel between her legs. And she exploded, the orgasm so powerful, she spasmed and gyrated, which caused tugging on her nipples and clit and the sensitive skin between her cheeks. Without even one moment to take a breath, she came again. Pleasure such as she'd never known rolled over her.

No way could she hold still. But Kane had stood,

placed his feet between hers, preventing her from closing her legs. And as she exploded, he kept caressing her with the towel, tugging the chain.

Powerful orgasms kept roaring through her, crashing over her. She thrashed and tried to buck and still he held her firm, cradling her with one arm, his breath in her ear, her chain wringing her dry.

And when she collapsed, he lifted her into his arms and carried her to the bed. She would not faint. She wanted to remember him holding her tenderly in his arms. She wanted to remember pressing her cheek to his chest and the feel of his solid heartbeat by her ear. She wanted to remember every detail of the entire lusty experience. Refusing to give in to the roaring in her ears or the narrowing of her vision, she fought to remain conscious with all her willpower.

And inch by inch she took back a measure of control. Slowly her breathing returned to normal. "I didn't know it was possible to experience so much pleasure."

"You have much to learn." As he spoke, the chain slid, tightening, taking up the slack from when she'd been bent over. But Kane hadn't touched her.

She looked from him to the chain at her breasts and back to him. "Did you make them do that?"

"I programmed them."

"They can readjust themselves?"

"The body buffs will detach the necessary sections whenever you use the bathroom, then reattach afterwards, of course."

He meant to keep her in the chain. However, recalling the pleasure she'd just experienced, she wasn't exactly upset. She eyed him across the pillow. "The buffs can attach the chain?"

"Didn't I just say so?"

She eyed his lips quirking with laughter and recalled him kneeling between her legs. "Then why did *you* attach them?"

"I couldn't deny myself."

So her shower had affected him after all. She couldn't have been more pleased by his admission. While he seemed in charge, he couldn't remain as collected as he pretended. She would keep working on him and sooner or later he was bound to give in. Meanwhile she fully intended to enjoy herself.

THE MORE TIME Kane spent with Fallon, the harder it was not to hold back. He wanted to tell her who he was and why he was here, but he wouldn't break his silence without a better reason than to protect himself from her. Besides, if she knew that there could never be anything between them beyond these few days, he doubted she would open herself so fully to being with him. Of course, even if he could be with her longer, he had no use for deeper emotions. As the phrase in this time went, *Been there. Done that.*

Nothing ate away at him like his mistake of falling hard for Cassandra during a mission. Never again would he allow a woman to interfere with an assignment. Cassandra! Even now he carried the short time they'd spent together locked in his heart. Lying to her through every day they'd spent together had almost killed him.

He refused to repeat the same mistake with Fallon. So Kane would continue to give her what he could during the time they would have together, but he would hold back any profound emotions. Because he was going to leave her. Their time together was limited by the length of his mission—as soon as he captured Nigel, he would return home.

However, he still intended to fulfill his promise. Fallon deserved a break from her responsibilities. He'd been monitoring her phone calls and already her sister had called twice, her mother and father once each and her secretary had three emergencies that someone else would have to handle. Fallon was incommunicado until he deemed otherwise, and that wouldn't be unless there was a life-threatening emergency. Her family had to learn to stand on their own.

He'd told himself he wouldn't become involved. Only he liked her. He liked her courage. He liked the way she looked him in the eye when she was shaking with raw need and allowed him to see how much she wanted him. And he liked the way she smelled.

No matter how many times he told himself he was heading for trouble, he couldn't seem to stop provoking her, especially when her every response was so delicious. Knowing better, knowing he'd been burned and would be again, couldn't keep him away from the heat of her flame. She simply burned too brightly for him to resist.

Knowing how much he would suffer after he departed didn't seem to be much of a deterrent. So he would enjoy their short time together. Make the most of every second, because eventually he would have to leave, and she must stay.

If he could have walked away from Fallon, he would have. But he couldn't make her that ill. It was no fault of hers that she'd become trapped with him in the stasis bubble for the duration of his mission. Yet, nevertheless, they had to deal with the fact that the bubble would collapse and eventually disintegrate and then shoot him back home. Before that happened, he had to stop Nigel from changing history.

Kane supposed the sooner he caught Nigel, the better for both Fallon and himself. And yet he was enjoying her company so much that he yearned to linger here.

But the laws of physics could not be changed. If he was going to catch Nigel, it must be soon.

However, they had time to eat and Kane ordered a huge breakfast that room service delivered to the suite. After they'd eaten croissants slathered in honey butter and topped with strawberry preserves, scrambled eggs with crisp bacon and fresh cantaloupe with raspberries, and washed the huge meal down with a pot of black coffee, Fallon reached across him for the phone.

"What are you doing?" he asked.

She raised a haughty brow. "Still don't trust me?"

"Answer the question."

"If we're attending the auction, I'll need to order some clothes."

"You will wear the chain."

She swept crumbs from the sheet across her chest and frowned at him. "I'll be arrested."

"Go stand in front of the mirror."

She sighed, but climbed out of bed and stepped in front of the full-length mirror. "All right. I'm here."

He focused for a moment on the body buff, sending directions how he wanted her dressed. "This is what you will wear."

Her lower jaw dropped. She appeared to be wearing a multicolored short dress and matching ankle boots.

"How—oh…my…" She spun around and glared at him. "My every move pulls on the chain."

He chuckled. "You're going to have a very interesting day."

"I won't be able to sit," she complained. "The chain is too tight."

"Sure you will. The body buff will adjust the chain to your needs."

"You forgot my panties."

"I didn't forget." He enjoyed her look of outrage and the sparkle of anticipation in her eyes. She might be protesting, but she was simply testing him.

"These auctions can go on for hours."

"Then I suggest you use your connections to arrange that the item you're going to buy for me is auctioned at the beginning of the sale."

"I don't have that kind of clout, and besides, who said I was buying anything for you?"

"What? You don't love me anymore?"

"Love you?" She glared at him. "I'm not even sure I like you."

"It doesn't matter as long as you want my hands on you," he teased. In truth, he didn't require her money. If she hadn't been caught in the stasis bubble with him for the duration of the mission, he would have made other arrangements to make the purchases he required. But the less unfamiliar technology she saw, the better. Kane was good at making use of what was available and that made him a valuable employee. The less material—and that included cash—he had to import from home, the less chance of his doing damage while he was here. Besides, Fallon had more money than she'd need in a hundred lifetimes. He grinned, watching her irritation turn to wonder as the buffs vibrated in all the right places.

"You don't play…fair." But there was no venom in her tone. In fact she was smiling as she tried not to squirm. But she couldn't help it. And as the vibrations aroused her, she moved, causing the chain to tug and her lips parted in a gasp.

He laughed, enjoying her pleasure. "Don't worry. I figure we can buy what I want for less than twenty-five million."

"Twenty-five…million?"

He adjusted the vibrations to work in tandem. Both nipples got attention, then her lower half, then her nipples once again. "That won't even put a dent in your net worth."

She sucked in her breath as she dealt with the sensations coursing through her. He had to give her credit: she was doing her damnedest to focus on the conversation. "What exactly am I buying?"

Though what he had to tell her would grab her attention, she wouldn't be able to ignore what was happening to her for long. She'd deprived herself of pleasure for so long that even the tiniest stimulation caused her pulse to increase and her eyes to dilate. Oh, yeah. This was going to be a very interesting day.

And he didn't know what he enjoyed more, surprising her with the technology or giving her an orgasm at the same time he delivered an answer. "We're buying a gadget that makes things invisible."

7

FALLON GASPED as a sizzling orgasm ripped through her. If Kane hadn't steadied her, she might have collapsed, climbed back into bed and dragged him with her. Instead she wobbled, and had barely recovered before he'd popped them over to Kendals in another of his mind-numbing instantaneous transporting moves.

His technology stunned her. She'd love to get her hands on a gadget that made objects invisible, but what really struck her were the infinite possibilities presented by the ability to travel at the speed of light. In a world where oil polluted and cost billions, securing the technology would allow nations to spend more money on health care and education.

The gadgets he'd attached to her body had their uses as well. Although she'd just enjoyed a fabulous orgasm, every step she took now tugged, stroked and stimulated, until she was certain she'd be ready for another very soon. She struggled to get control as they left the private alcove at Kendals. Kane had dressed himself in a white shirt, suit and tie that did wonders to make him appear sophisticated and he easily fit in with the wealthy crowd.

Kendals held their auctions in an enormous ballroom and Fallon had worked with the firm many times to raise money for the Hanover Institute. Even her wealth could not solely fund the research required to find the cure for cancer. As a previous customer she recognized the raised stage with video cameras and large-screen monitors, which would show off everything from diamonds to art to the people who sat in the very last row of chairs in the audience. Although she'd been here before, Fallon didn't often come to Kendals in person. She lacked the time and usually skimmed the catalogue ahead of time and either bid anonymously by phone or instructed one of her executive assistants to bid for her.

However, this auction was a bit different than most. Silent and anonymous bids weren't being accepted, and the items today weren't the usual rare art, silk carpets or estate items such as antiques or jewelry. Today was all about technology. Patents, prototypes of innumerable gadgets, computer slide presentations and all sorts of catalogues were displayed along the room's perimeter in booths.

She and Kane strolled along the displays. While most items didn't interest her, she admired a pair of prototype sunglasses that required no wires to run the built-in cell phone and MP3 technology. Another item she thought had merit was a quartz kitchen countertop with antibacterial properties.

However, concentrating on the displays in the booths was almost impossible. Kane's buffs kept distracting her. And those rings and the chain rippling across her skin had her anxious to sit before she worked herself up again. Although she'd nodded hello and kissed the air next to a few women's faces, she'd avoided conversation as much as possible. While she was aware of speculation about Kane, she didn't stop to chat or introduce him. He seemed too bent on finding the display he wanted to notice a number of women sizing him up.

Several times they got separated when acquaintances stopped her and he moved on, but each time, she felt an inner tug that told her the distance between them was becoming too great. And she hadn't forgotten if she didn't stay close by, she would become ill again. Still, it was her nature to test her limits so she experimented to discover exactly how far away she could safely go from him. She was disturbed to find, just as Kane had predicted, her margin of safety from illness was about one third less distance than when she'd tried to run away from him in the parking garage.

Not only was she aware of her proximity to Kane, she was very aware of him as a man. Although women admired him and several introduced themselves, he moved on quickly. She never saw Kane speak to anyone with real interest and she found herself pleased. She wanted him all to herself. He seemed focused solely on the job right now, though, completely unaware of her—until she caught him glance across the room and catch her eye.

The zing of that connection startled her. Kane was a man on a mission and yet, he'd found time to make sure he kept up his end of the bargain. And she found herself wondering for the first time what he thought of her. Was he enjoying their little games? Did he want to make love to her as much as she wanted him to?

She'd seen physical evidence of his desire for her, but clearly, he was holding back physically and emotionally. And although she'd thought a fling would satisfy her, she now admitted to herself that she wanted so much more. While the orgasms were terrific, she wanted to know about Kane. The mystery surrounding him, which she'd found exciting and provoking, was now stopping them from moving into a deeper relationship.

She recognized that lurking beneath the surface was a growing emotional connection between them. Even in this crowded room, she was so aware of him—and not just physically. At a shared glance, she could tell that right now business was on his mind.

When Dan Mitchell, Kendals' chief auctioneer welcomed her and asked what she might be interested in today, she glanced across the room to see Kane in deep conversation with a man she recognized—Logan Kincaid, head of the Shey Group, an ultrasecret group of ex-CIA, FBI and military specialists who took on high-risk missions for the U.S. government, private corporations and individuals for very large sums of money.

Kane's discussion with Kincaid immediately aroused her curiosity and she quickly ended her conversation with Mitchell and approached Kane. She gritted her teeth as the chains tugged and aroused, strolling as quickly as she dared toward the two men, wondering if Kane could possibly work for the Shey Group. She hoped so. Logan Kincaid was a patriot who'd risked his life many times over for his country. He'd been with NSA and helped write the code for the antimissile defense system. There were rumors he had a direct line into the White House as well as the Kremlin and since he possessed close ties to the CIA, she wondered if he could check out Kane for her on an unofficial basis.

As she joined the two men, both men acknowledged her presence, Kane by placing a possessive hand on her waist, an action that yanked the chain. She had to bite back a gasp of pleasure as she nodded a greeting to Kincaid.

Kane's tone was respectful, yet jocular. "So Fallon's trustworthy?"

She'd been thinking about asking Kincaid the same question about Kane. To find the two men discussing her loyalty unnerved her. What the hell was going on?

Kincaid didn't break a smile, but intelligent eyes revealed his amusement that Kane would question her loyalty right in front of her. "Fallon's proven her worth and her allegiance many times over."

Fallon didn't know if the men were talking in code or pulling her leg. But her devotion to her country and the Agency had never been questioned and the fact that Kane was doing so right in front of her was not only irritating and outrageous, but revealing. As much as she wanted to slap Kane upside the head, she found the camaraderie between these two men reassuring.

If Kane was up to no good, Kincaid would likely be aware of it. She wondered how much he knew about Kane's mission and why they were here today.

Kane tightened his grip on her waist. "So I'm free to tell her my secrets?"

Kane had phrased his question casually, yet she sensed he was asking permission. Again she wondered if he worked for Kincaid or his organization, but she kept her lips pressed firmly together. Now was not the time. Too many people around them could eavesdrop.

Logan Kincaid clapped Kane on the back and laughed. "I'd say that's up to you. But any man who tells a woman all his secrets is either a fool or in love." The smile never left his face, but his tone changed. "You aren't a fool and you cannot afford to fall in love."

"I'll keep that in mind." Kane nodded and together Fallon and he ambled away from Kincaid.

"You two know one another?" she asked as they stopped in front of a blueprint of a robot that could iron clothes. After glancing at the prototype's five-million dollar price tag, Fallon moved on. Interesting idea, but at that high a price, the robot wouldn't replace dry cleaning anytime soon.

"We're related. Didn't I mention my last name is Kincaid?"

"No. You didn't." The two men shared dark hair and both had broad shoulders and fit bodies. But their features were nothing alike. "How are you related?"

"He's my great-great-grandfather."

"What?" That was impossible. She stopped. His hand tugged but she ignored the chain dancing along her nerve endings. "Logan Kincaid can't be more than thirty-five."

"He's thirty-seven."

Fallon's thoughts swam through what seemed like a sea of mud. Kane had already told her he'd fallen in love with a woman who'd gone on to become a grandmother. If he wasn't lying, and after the technology she'd seen, she didn't think he was, then he had to be from the future. And obviously Logan Kincaid knew it. Perhaps that's why he'd come by today, since he hadn't remained to bid.

Was time travel possible? Could people in the future come back in time? Fallon's mind swirled at the possibility. She had dozens of questions, but Kane was making a beeline to one of the booths. He must have found what he was looking for.

At first so many people stood close by that she couldn't see the technology that made objects turn invisible. But as the line moved slowly forward, between two security guards she glimpsed a glowing round crystal cylinder. When a man pressed a switch, a vase with flowers disappeared and the crystal's glow dimmed. Around her people marveled, oohed and aahed.

One man told his wife he wasn't buying an elaborate magic trick. Several men asked to see the paperwork and the security guard told them the engineering would be sold with the product. Fallon had no idea if this was standard procedure but she applauded Kendals' precautions.

She could imagine many military applications and shuddered. An enemy could make invisible bombs and leave them anywhere. The U.S. would have few defenses against what couldn't be seen, and she wondered why her government was allowing this auction to take place.

"How large an item can be made invisible?" she asked Kane.

"A crystal that size could make me invisible for a year." He kept his voice low and turned her toward the seats. "We have to win the bid."

Fallon didn't like the idea of spending her money on a gadget that could be turned into a weapon. And yet, better the CIA had it than fanatical enemies. Ever since Kane's conversation with Logan Kincaid, she'd suppressed the dozens of questions she had about Kane and his mission, but she didn't like being kept in the dark. If she was going to purchase such an expensive and dangerous item, she wanted to be fully briefed. She wanted all her brain cells to focus on the task at hand.

As she realized that she wanted to concentrate on business, not pleasure, she noted that the buffs were no longer stimulating her. The chain was still attached to her skin, but so loose it no longer distracted her. So Kane had told her the truth. The body buffs would only do what she welcomed. And when she truly didn't want to be aroused, they deactivated.

She may not have caught Kane in even one tiny lie, but she knew he was holding out on her. She couldn't make good decisions when he kept her in the dark.

As she took a seat beside him, she caught the glances of several people who seemed more than casually interested in Kane—and they weren't all women. One was a man with blond hair, green eyes and an icy stare.

She nudged Kane. "See that blond man to your right?" Just as she spoke the blonde ducked out of the room.

"Who?"

"Never mind." She shook her head. "The guy seemed to be taking too much interest in you."

Kane opened his shirt pocket and plucked out a 3-D picture. "This him?"

She studied the image. Never had she seen such crisp detail, clearer than her high-definition television set—only it wasn't a flat image, but a hologram. In the image, the man possessed the same cold green eyes, but his hair was short and black. And he wore a beard.

"I think it's the same guy, but I'm not certain. Is this Nigel?"

"Yes. First we'll purchase the technology and then I'll catch him."

Kane made the statement as if there was no

chance of failure, no other way his mission could finish. If she hadn't seen Nigel's eyes, she wouldn't have had so many doubts. But the lack of humanity in his soulless stare made her shiver.

."Cold?"

"It doesn't bother you that Nigel knows you're here?"

"He knew I would come after him. Now he can't run again until he sells the technology."

"Why not?"

"He needs the money."

Kane's thinking was simple—too simple—and she felt obligated to point out his mistake. "Nigel can have the money transferred by wire. He needn't stick around to collect. By the time we purchase and finish with the paperwork, he could zap himself to China."

"There's no place he can go that we cannot follow."

If Kane had meant to reassure her, he hadn't. His plan made no sense to her. Either he didn't understand all the ways Nigel could disappear or Kane was holding back information again. She suspected the latter.

They really needed to talk. But with the seats around them filling in and the auctioneer starting the bidding, now was not the time. Fallon bid on the innovative sunglasses and won, then lost out when she dropped out of the bidding on the quartz countertops.

Although she kept out a sharp eye for Nigel, she

didn't see him again. Not even when the crystal that turned objects invisible went up for sale. The auctioneer explained that only the winning bidder would see the plans, the patent and the engineering. If the winner wasn't completely satisfied, he or she would have twenty-four hours to return the item and it would go to today's second-highest bidder.

The bidding began at five million and quickly escalated to twelve. Fallon had yet to raise the paddle with her bid number on it. She never jumped in too early, getting a feel for the other bidders and the rhythm of the sale. Next to her, Kane didn't flinch a muscle or change expression, but then it wasn't his money they were spending.

The bidding slowed at fifteen million. Daron Levenger, a financial analyst from Price Dunstreet kept up a steady conversation with someone on his cell phone while Daisy Malone, a European investor whose fortune originated in Swiss banks, hesitated to raise her bid. While she deliberated, Fallon finally jumped her bid straight to twenty million, hoping the other two bidders would drop out.

Daisy bit her bottom lip and shook her head as Fallon had hoped. But then Daron went to twenty-two. And a new bidder entered the fray, Jamaal Ali Azeez, his wealth grounded in Saudi oil, coming in at twenty-five million.

Fallon didn't like Jamaal. As far as she was concerned the hypocrite should go back to his homeland and his five wives, fifteen children and thirty-three grandchildren. His lifestyle irritated her for several reasons. A man who had five wives shouldn't be cheating on them with his French mistress, but Jamaal did it openly and proudly. She liked his political leanings even less. He had ties to poppy fields in Afghanistan that terrorists turned into heroin, which they sold to fund their illegal activities, and it was rumored he had several congressmen in his hip pocket. No, she had no use for Jamaal, but the man was far wealthier than she and could outbid her if he wished.

"Perhaps you should have asked your great-great-grandfather to stay," she muttered to Kane.

"Why?"

She bid again, trying to decide how high she was willing to go. "He can better afford this purchase."

"Bidder thirty-seven bids thirty million," the auctioneer went on with his singsong patter.

At her comment, Kane rolled his eyes to the ceiling. "Is spending money so painful for you?"

"Wasting money is painful," she snapped, irritated when Jamaal went to thirty-two million. She immediately jumped to thirty-five. She didn't want him to sense any weakness. While she was prepared to go to at least forty, she had already spent more than she'd planned for an item she didn't want.

Jamaal hesitated, then shook his head. Finally the auctioneer dropped the gavel. "Sold for thirty-five million dollars to Ms. Fallon Hanover. And that concludes our auction. Thank you all for coming."

FALLON SETTLED HER BILL and accepted the crystal and plans. Kane waited for a private moment then transferred them back to the hotel room. While Fallon used the bathroom, he placed the plans in a garbage can, lit a match and began to burn them.

Fallon rushed back into the living area, her eyes wide, her steps at a run. She tried to take the can with the burning papers from him. "What are you doing?"

"I always intended to destroy these items." He held the can out of her reach and when the smoke detector was about to sound off, he used his specialized technology to prevent it.

She picked up the crystal and held it out to him. "I just paid a small fortune for this…thing. If we're going to destroy it, I deserve to know everything."

He had to admire her intelligence. She hadn't tried to stop him after her first burst of horror. Not that she could have stopped him from doing what he aimed to but that knowledge wouldn't have prevented most people from trying. Instead, she was facing the fact that his action might be a good one and was asking for an explanation.

"You might want to sit down." The papers quickly finished burning and he stirred the ashes with a hanger, then washed them down the sink drain at the bar.

"You're from the future, aren't you?" she demanded, without taking a seat. Instead she fixed them both a drink of tomato juice, vodka and a celery stick and he noted that her hands weren't even shaking.

He'd given her enough clues to guess the truth. Still, she had to be shocked. In his own time, only a few civilians had heard of time travel. Only those who served the government and needed to know ever learned about the technology.

"Yes. I'm from the future. I traveled in a time bubble and you were caught in it. The illness you experienced is on a cellular level. There are no permanent harmful effects, but you are trapped with me for the duration of my mission."

"Which is?"

"Nigel James is also from the future. He stole technology and is trying to sell it here."

She bit into her celery stick, chewed and swallowed. "I'm assuming he's under the same constraints you are? He'll eventually return to the future, also?"

Kane nodded. "But we couldn't wait to catch him in our future. Allowing him to sell those items would disturb the time line. The consequences could be catastrophic."

"How?"

"Without being too specific, suppose," he took the crystal from her, opened the power source and disconnected the battery, "the wrong people got hold of this item? They could change history by planting a bomb in the Oval Office."

"So I spent millions of dollars to—"

"Preserve the status quo."

"The Agency could do a lot of good with that crystal."

"Perhaps." He tossed it into the air and caught it. Before she said more, he placed it on the floor, crushed it with his shoes, then ground every memory chip to dust before sweeping it into the trashcan. "But this machine isn't supposed to be here. Even if your people used it for good, it could still damage the time line."

"And who are you to decide what's good for my world?" she demanded, her tone ringing with real annoyance.

"You're forgetting that I've seen the future and it's—"

"Perfect?"

"Better than now."

She crossed her arms across her chest. "That's too vague for me."

"I'm not allowed to be more specific. I shouldn't be telling you this much. Just the knowledge that the future is a better place might change your actions and damage the time line."

"What do you mean?"

"Perhaps if you're optimistic about the future, you'll invest more heavily in computer circuits or transistors, instead of oil. With your buying power, you could change economies, alter the market."

She shook her head. "You're giving me way too much credit. But I have another question. If Nigel is going back to your time, how will he take his new-found wealth with him?"

"There are several possibilities. For example, he could convert his paper wealth to a commodity and leave it in a trust. Or he could hide it and retrieve it in the future."

"Has this kind of unofficial time travel happened before?" she asked.

"A few times. I'm a time cop. It's my job to pre-serve history."

"And it was during one of your past missions that you fell in love?"

He held her gaze. "I left without a trace and she never knew why."

"My...God." She raised a hand to her lips, her eyes bright with compassion. "You never told her?"

"She lived in a time without much technology. And back then I never broke the rules."

She eyed him with a speculative arch of her brow. "And if Kincaid hadn't cleared me, you wouldn't be telling me, either."

At her words, his frustration escalated. He could not go through falling in love and leaving a woman again. And there was a reason he'd been harsh and uncom-municative: to discourage her and to protect himself. "If you know the truth and understand that I must leave, you will not allow your emotions to become involved."

She let out a long, low whistle. "Damn you. It's too late. You should have told me sooner."

"I will not allow you to have feelings for me."

"Really?" She released a harsh laugh. "Do you have a machine, some new invention in that future of yours, to prevent people from having feelings?"

"That's not what I meant. I've been so reserved and distant, there should never have been any real connection between us." And if the time bubble hadn't trapped them together, they wouldn't even be having this conversation.

"Maybe you've held back with words. But your actions and expressions reveal the real you. From the first moment we met, when you handed me a damp paper towel to ease my sickness, you've shown yourself to be kind. You also like to be in control. The pleasure I've had has all been very one-sided, no doubt so you could keep your feelings in check." He stared at her, surprised she could know him so well. She sighed again. "Well, did it work?"

"What?"

"Did stopping yourself from making love to me prevent you from wanting to?"

"Of course not."

"So—" she shoved a lock of hair behind her ear and drilled him with a stare "—what you're telling me is that your rationale for not making love to me is a complete failure." She held out her hands to him. "And since you've already broken your rules by revealing your secret to me, you might as well break the rest of them."

His mouth went dry. She was offering him everything he wanted…everything he couldn't have.

8

KANE SHOT FALLON a harsh, heated look that should have rocked her back on her heels and made her wish she'd never uttered those last words. "You want to make love to me, knowing that after I leave in a few days it will be impossible for us ever to see one another again?"

Fallon didn't hesitate. "If we don't make love, I will regret it for the rest of my life."

He countered. "And if we do, you may regret it for the rest of your life."

She grinned, her smile saucy, her hip cocked at a brazen angle. "If we could have regrets either way, then why not enjoy ourselves today?"

Kane chuckled, pulling out her cell phone and offering it to her. "You certain you wouldn't rather return these dozens of phone calls?"

He was testing her. And she almost reached for the phone out of habit, but she resisted and shook her head. "What I want right now is you."

"Your mom's called eight times."

"Then she's still alive, and right now, that's all I need to know. But what about you? What about catching Nigel?"

"He's already gone." Kane's tone was light and easy as if catching Nigel didn't matter, but she knew he was not a man to take his mission lightly.

"How do you know he's gone?"

"I can…keep track of him."

Kane was being vague and she realized he was trying hard not to reveal more about the future technology. But if he could track Nigel, then why had he earlier insisted on using the television to find him? Did his technology require the television for it to work? "So you know where he is?"

Kane shook his head. "I should have said I am aware of his proximity to me, just like you are aware of when I'm near you."

She didn't understand. "But you and I are connected through the time bubble."

"Our connection to one another is different," he admitted, then let out a long, low breath of air. "All you need to know is that when Nigel uses our technology, I'm aware of it. And once he discovered that we'd spotted him, I had the choice of either following him or securing the technology. Since the technology was dangerous, I had no choice but to let him go."

"So where is he now?"

"He jumped from New York to Logan airport. I haven't picked him up since then. He must have taken commercial transportation after that."

"Perhaps I can be of some assistance." She held out her hand. "My cell phone, please."

He passed it to her without hesitation and she was pleased to see that he trusted her more than he had before. She dialed Dan Mitchell, Kendals' chief auctioneer. "Dan, I'd like to know the seller's name of the item I purchased today."

"I'm sorry that information is private."

"Dan, I'd consider it a personal favor. And you know I can be discreet."

At her words, Kane raised an eyebrow. Let him wonder. She wasn't about to explain how last year her intoxicated mother had palmed a million-dollar brooch out from under Kendals' security guards' noses. Fallon had returned the item and no one had ever known about their security lapse or her mother's indiscretion.

"Art Drayson? Okay. Thanks, Dan. I owe you one."

"One what?" Kane asked.

"It's just an expression. Another way to say thanks."

Fallon dialed her personal assistant next. "Janet."

"Oh, thank God. Your mother wanted me to call the FBI and report you'd been kidnapped. You all right?"

"I'm fine. I need you to—"

"Your sister was arrested last night and her lawyer won't bail her out until—"

"Not now."

"But your mother is hysterical."

"Janet, I need you to call my travel agent. A Mr. Art Drayson departed Logan airport this morning. I want you to find him for me."

"Yes, ma'am. What do you want me to do about—"

"Tell them I'm at a high-level conference and cannot be disturbed. I've got to go." Fallon hung up before Janet could tell her about any other emergencies and she gave in. The more time she spent away from the constant business of her life, the more she realized that she allowed her family too much leeway. Jaycee had already been trying to tell her that she wasn't responsible for everyone else, but letting go was hard. It was her nature to fix problems, to help. Perhaps her good intentions with her family had made them dependent on her. Without her there to fix things, maybe they'd learn to cope on their own. And no matter how difficult it was for her to let go, this was the perfect opportunity to allow her family and employees to stand up for themselves. She'd spent years building an efficient organization and had good people in place. If she let them run things for a day, surely the Hanover empire wouldn't fall apart. Surely the research for a cure for cancer wouldn't end. And it might do her sister some good to spend a night in jail—maybe then she'd admit she had a problem and get some help.

Fallon tossed the cell phone back to Kane and was surprised by how liberating it felt to be rid of the machine that kept her at the beck and call of others. "Janet will find Nigel and call back."

"Do you know you're amazing?" Approval glowed in his eyes and she sucked in her breath as his heat washed over her.

"For helping you find Nigel?" she asked.

"For getting what you want."

"Excuse me?"

"You cleared my calendar and yours. So we have nothing to do for a while." He eyed her with a look she couldn't read, as if he was thinking five steps ahead.

"That's a good thing, right?" She was suddenly a bit less sure of herself. Perhaps she should have allowed herself to be satisfied with orgasms orchestrated by gadgets. Perhaps she'd been wrong to long for Kane's personal involvement. But just thinking about him kissing her and holding her made her pulse leap with excitement.

"You know it suddenly occurred to me that you are wearing way too many clothes." He fingered the tied shoulder strap of her dress and it unfastened as if by magic. Then the whole dress disappeared, leaving her standing before him in nothing but gold glitter, the dangling chain and spiked heels. "Ah, better."

Although she'd spent a good part of her time with him in an undressed state, the suddenness of losing her clothes while he remained fully dressed reminded her of how much personal control she'd ceded to him. And as much as she wanted to fling herself into his arms, unbutton his shirt and tear off his slacks, she'd agreed to yield control of the direction and timing of their touching to him.

The rings attached to her most sensitive places were dormant now. However, she suspected from the gleam in Kane's eyes that wouldn't be the case for long.

"Come here." His tone went husky, making her steps to obey him shaky and difficult.

But she held her chin high. Didn't rush. In fact, she managed to sway her hips a little more than necessary. But she paid for that sway when the chain tugged and a tingling jolt arced through her flesh.

"It also occurred to me that I haven't introduced you to the discipline of remaining still while I taste you."

Desire rippled through her. "I am ready to do whatever you ask."

"Are you?"

"Yes."

"Do not move."

He dipped his head and she thought for certain he would kiss her lips. But he didn't. Instead, he bent farther, until his breath fanned her breast. With almost no warning he took half her breast into his mouth and the exquisite warmth and his clever tongue flicking over her nipple caused her to gasp.

She almost reached out and clutched his shoulders to steady herself, but just in time remembered to hold still. And then her eyes closed at the wonder of his lips and tongue laving her breast, tugging on the ring of her nipple. And suddenly the pleasant tingling began to pulse, as if his mouth had activated a totally new sensation. Her breast became more sensitive than she'd ever imagined. Each cell vibrated with energy that reverberated deep inside her and thrummed in rhythm to her heartbeat.

And when he switched his mouth to her other breast, the delicious sensations began all over again. Standing became an effort.

She longed to reach out, clutch the back of his head and thread her fingers through his hair. At the same time, she wondered how much longer she could remain still. And just when she thought that she might pool into a puddle, he took her nipple between his teeth and lightly bit her.

"Ow," she complained.

But when he sucked away the tiny pain and wondrous heat flooded through her, she gasped in awe. "I've never felt…anything so…incredible."

He moved to bite her other nipple. "If you move… I'm going to start over."

"Start ov—oh…my…" His words hit her at the same time as the heat. No mere mouth or tongue— no matter how skillful—could be teasing and taunting her like he was. He had to be manipulating her through the rings and chain attached to her flesh. But between feeling the delicious sensations coursing through her and willing her muscles not to move, she couldn't think clearly. But one thing she knew for certain: she couldn't stand still too much longer. Yet the idea of him beginning the sweet torture all over again kept her motionless, trembling, wanting.

"My legs won't support me much longer," she warned him. "You feel too good."

"I'm just getting started."

He couldn't be serious. She'd never been more ready to make love. She wanted him inside her. Now. She wanted his flesh against hers. Now. She wanted him to be pumping back and forth as frantically as her own heartbeat. Now.

But he, as usual, was in complete control, albeit breathing a little heavily. And as lovely as the anticipation zinging through her was, she simply wasn't accustomed to this intense stimulation.

"Kane, please. I am...oh...oh...trying to do... what you ask, but I am not...used to...I cannot—"

She didn't think it was possible, but she was going to orgasm from his touching her breasts and only her breasts—but then he lifted his head and his gaze seared her. "This is what you wanted."

"I wanted to make love."

"You said I would set the terms."

Her breasts ached, her nipples hard as her thoughts swirled. "I didn't know waiting could be so..." She licked her bottom lip, trying to find the right word. "I didn't know waiting could be so difficult."

He checked his watch and she wanted to smack him. "It's only been a few minutes."

He had to be wrong. She was going to explode. Her pulse was racing. Her legs trembling. She was slick and ready. Delaying longer would do nothing but irritate her. "What are you waiting for?"

His stare bored into her, demanding that she understand. "It is not your right to question me. However, if you cannot support yourself, I will solve that problem."

She expected him to lead her to the bed, or a sofa, or a chair. Instead, he picked up a stool and set it on the desk, then placed his hands on her waist and lifted her until she sat on the stool, her heels on the desk.

"Part your legs."

Excitement raced through her. But then she realized that making love in this position wasn't likely. Obviously, he intended to keep right on teasing her.

"My mouth is going to trace every inch of those chains," he promised.

She didn't see how. The chain went directly between her legs and she was sitting on part of it. But she opened her legs and when he reached between her thighs, she prayed that his touch would give her a measure of relief from the need holding her strung so tightly.

Instead, he yanked out the stool from beneath her. She let out a shout, expecting to fall. But she didn't. He'd suspended her in the air over the desk. Totally open to him, she instinctively tried to close her legs—and couldn't.

"What have you done?" she asked.

"You no longer have to worry about supporting your weight," he told her, offering no explanation at all.

She couldn't close her legs. Couldn't stand. Couldn't run. Her hands rested on her parted thighs. She couldn't move them, either.

"In fact, since you can no longer move," he grinned at her predicament while he tweaked both her nipples between thumbs and forefingers, "you are totally at my mercy."

She was naked, totally helpless and all she could think about was that her nipples wanted more of the same. She was craving his touch like an addict. But she could do nothing but wait for whatever he did. And despite that she craved his touch, he looked so damned satisfied and smug with his bright-eyed expression that if she could have closed her legs, she would have. "I'll let you do whatever you want."

"Now, you no longer have a choice."

She swallowed hard as he pointed out the subtle difference. It was one thing to yield to him. It was totally different to be entirely at his mercy. And her body was wringing with need, trembling at the idea that he could touch her, where, when and how he liked and she could do no more than wait and anticipate.

And when he tilted her position in midair, he did it slowly, thoroughly enjoying her realization that her most private parts were now tipping up toward his face. His gaze focused on her neatly shaved mons, then lower to her lips dusted with golden sparkles, and finally to her pulsing clit that he'd branded with his rings and chain.

And she'd never felt so wanton, so wanted. She could see his desire reflected in his eyes. See how alluring he found her. And then his mouth seared a path up her leg. He nibbled and nipped and she gasped and would have squirmed or pulled his head closer. But she could do nothing—except enjoy every lick, every nibble as he edged ever closer to where she wanted him most.

"You like having to wait on me…don't you?" he asked, his tone low and husky, leaving no doubt he was totally enjoying himself.

"Yes."

"You even like it when I don't give you what you think you want. Correct?" he demanded.

"Yes." As much as she hated to admit he was right, she couldn't lie when his mouth was so intimately pressed to the inside of her thigh. She was quivering with the need for release, but he wasn't in any hurry at all. His hands cupped her bottom, his fingers tracing up and down the chain and driving her as wild as his lips and his tongue, which finally landed exactly where she wanted.

He seemed to know exactly what she needed to reach orgasm but deliberately denied her. His lips and tongue teased and taunted. She was panting, feeling so much tension that she would have been shaking with it if he hadn't trapped her there by unknown forces.

When her phone rang, she figured he'd ignore it. She damn sure intended to. If only he'd increase the pressure of his wondrous licks on her most sensitive flesh. But no, he pulled the cell from her purse and left her aching. "We don't need to talk to anyone right now," she complained.

"But it's Janet." He smiled wickedly. "She may have information about Nigel."

She could think of nothing but him putting his mouth back where it had been before the phone call and her frustration escalated. "I'll call her back."

"Talk to her now." He held the phone to her ear with one hand. His other plunged straight into her heat.

"Helloooooh." She practically moaned into the phone.

"I found him."

Kane's fingers moved cleverly over her clit, rubbing the ring, and a current sizzled along the chains all the way up to her sensitive nipples, making it almost impossible to think.

Oh my… He was going to make her come. Right while she…she had to wait. "Where is he?"

"Vegas."

She had to get off the phone fast. "Send me the hotel and room number."

"Where are you?"

Kane replaced his fingers with his tongue and she almost screamed. "Text message me."

"Okay. You have a call from—"

"Bye." Without her hands free, she couldn't hang up. Luckily Kane did it for her. But he also straightened to do so, once again denying her completion. She glared at him. "You're insane. How could you do that to me when I was on the—"

"Did you want me to stop?" He was laughing at her, totally enjoying his domination.

She was so hot, she could barely form words and sputtered, "I didn't want you to stop, but you have."

"So you want me to continue with my insanity?"

He was teasing her and all she wanted was to reach for his hips, tear off his clothes, wrap her legs around him and draw him closer. But she couldn't move. Couldn't even squirm as he raked her with his gaze, ending with a hungry stare between her legs.

One glance at the gleam in his eyes and her irritation died, replaced by a lovely glow of anticipation.

He raised his eyes to meet hers, then slowly inserted one finger into her warmth and rested his thumb lightly on her clit. Between his heated stare and his skillful hands, he made the gesture gentle and intimate as well as erotic, and all kinds of heat flowed into her.

"You know why you are enjoying yourself so much?" he asked, his voice filled with lazy tension.

She had no idea. She didn't want to talk or think. All her energy focused on his sliding thumb and the delicious stirring of her senses.

When she didn't answer, he tapped her clit.

"Ah," she sighed, knowing she needed more to find release and wondering how long he would hold her right on the delicious edge.

"Well?" His voice deepened.

"I need more. But I want to come with you inside me."

"Why?" He tapped her clit several times, then stopped, waiting for her answer.

"It'll be better."

"Why?"

"Sharing…ah…pleasure…oh…is better."

"Wrong answer." He withdrew his hand.

She was quivering, trembling, and had to bite her bottom lip to keep from screaming at him as ever so slowly the heat he'd built receded and the roaring in her ears ebbed.

When she could finally speak, she forced words past her lips. "Why did you stop?"

His stare pierced her. "You wanted to give me pleasure or you wanted to take back control?"

She would have shrugged if she could have moved. Her thoughts swirled but she sensed her answer was important to him. She shut her eyes so she could think. Why *did* she want to make love? Did she truly want to give him pleasure or did she want to take back some control?

"I don't know," she told him, opening her eyes. "I'm not the kind of person simply to take pleasure and not give back."

"But I want you only to take. Watching you yield gives me pleasure. And you just denied me."

His words made her chest hitch. "But…but… don't you want my touch? Don't you want to make love and have an orgasm?"

"You still don't understand. You are not responsible for my enjoyment. What I want, I will take. What I want, I will demand."

He wanted her to do absolutely nothing but what he asked, not even give him something in return. No wait. Her total submission would be his pleasure. He was enjoying her submission more than she'd realized. But what frightened and thrilled her right down to her toes was the freedom of doing as he demanded. She wasn't responsible for his pleasure or her own. It was all about enjoying the moment. She didn't have to do one little thing and the concept was so absolutely selfish that she had never even thought of it.

With him in control the sex was all about her. He was giving her…everything. All she had to do was accept.

She raised her gaze to his. "I didn't truly understand until now. Thank you."

"You're welcome." The nod of his head was almost imperceptible, but his eyes darkened with pleasure. A rakish grin twitched his mouth into a crooked line.

And then he spun her over in the air until her forehead and knees were almost touching the desk. With her hands on her thighs and her legs still parted, her bottom was now tipped upward. She could no longer see him, but from the heat on her bottom he still stood over her, looking at every inch of exposed flesh.

She held her breath, wondering what he would do. Very consciously she let go of her embarrassment and vulnerability to embrace the pleasure he would give her. He rested his hand on her bottom, lightly played with the chain that tugged on her breasts and her clit and every sensitive place in between.

She couldn't hold back a moan of pleasure as every single nerve in her fired and demanded more. But with no idea what he would do next, she could only wait.

She heard him drag a chair to the desk, and the leather creaked as he took a seat. Once again he fingered her chain, but almost absentmindedly, lightly, not enough to come close to giving her release.

She suspected she no longer had his full attention but it didn't matter. She was longing for an orgasm and if he chose to give her one, then she would be happy for it. And if he chose to delay, somehow she would enjoy that, too. Because as he booted the computer beside her, she was learning that his forcing her patience was upping her enjoyment. Every tiny stroke of his hand, every slight tug of the chain brought more and more excitement. He was winding her up like a top and it was only a matter of time before he spun her out of control.

"Janet is right. Nigel is in Vegas. He's made reservations to stay there for four days. Apparently potential buyers can view the items for sale at the hotel, but that's not until tomorrow, so we needn't rush."

"Good." She couldn't believe he was talking to her about business while fondling her so intimately.

"And if we're going to keep this up, we'll need nourishment." He picked up the phone, but his hand brushed over her mons and she sucked in her breath, realizing she'd never been so sensitive. "What would you like?"

"Touch me there again."

"I meant what would you like for me to order for you to eat?"

"I'm not hungry for food."

He laughed. "If you faint on me, it's not going to be from hunger but from the pleasure."

And then he proceeded to order a veritable feast. She was certain she wouldn't be able to eat one bite. Her nerves were ragged from wondering what he would do next, where he would touch her next. And when he would—if ever he would—give her another orgasm.

Instead, he seemed intent on stroking her back,

her breasts and bottom, once again totally ignoring the needy area between her legs. She should have been totally relaxed on her bed of air, but instead her muscles drew tight and her belly clenched. Her position left her unable to see him but she could imagine his pleasure as she quivered at his every caress.

When room service knocked, she expected him to free her. The chair scraped over the carpet and he stood and stepped away, his steps fading. She held her breath, listening to hear if he'd at least shut the door. He didn't.

While the suite's office was around the corner from the front door which he would open, just the idea of waiting here while he allowed someone else to come inside made her realize even more fully that she had no control over the matter. Recalling how he hadn't wanted her stepbrother to see one exposed inch of her flesh, she forced air into her lungs.

But she couldn't stop thinking about how she would look to anyone coming through that door. With her bottom tipped up and her legs parted, she was exposed to the max. And she was more excited than she'd ever been in her life.

Because she trusted Kane. Totally trusted him with her body. Trusted him to understand her better than she understood herself.

She listened intently to hear whether room service had left. But she couldn't tell. She heard a cart rolling into the room. Smelled hot croissants, cheeses, fruits, coffee and wine. Suspecting Kane had returned alone, but uncertain, she found her mouth had gone dry—even as moisture seeped between her thighs.

Kane chuckled. "So, you're happy I'm back?"

"Yes."

He pulled out the chair. And he spun her again, this time she landed in his lap, facing him, her legs dangling to either side of his knees. The transition stunned her. The blood that had gone to her brain rushed to her lower limbs.

She caught sight of her reflection in a mirror over his shoulder. Cheeks flushed, eyes dilated, her hair mussed, she looked pouty and soft and feminine— and needy, with her nipples hard and pointy beneath the gold glitter. But it was the chain that made her look sexy as hell. A chain that she wore proudly for him.

Her gaze went to his. No way could she eat unless he released the knots in her belly, eased the fiery desire coursing through her veins. And as much as she wanted an orgasm, she realized she wanted something more.

Never had anyone paid so much attention to her. Never had any man read her better than she knew herself. He was allowing her to be utterly selfish.

But she wanted more. Not just an orgasm—although she'd never needed one more than she did at the moment. He'd revved her up until she was ready to explode with no more than a caress. But her response to him was more than physical, she was opening to him emotionally. She could feel a mental shifting, an awakening that she'd shut down after her divorce.

So even though she craved release, even more she craved him to want her as much as she wanted him.

9

KANE THOUGHT she finally understood that he took pleasure from watching her. Oh, he fully intended to satisfy both of them. Just not quite yet. She was having too much fun, perhaps for the first time in years, for him to cut short the experience. He wanted her to feel every nuance of arousal.

And as much as he wanted to continue to touch her fabulous silky skin, breathe in her essence and cause her flesh to quiver, he needed to allow her a measure of calm—just so he could build her back up again.

Besides, he liked having her on his lap, naked. And when he thought of all the pleasure he had yet to give her, his heart quickened in anticipation. Now that he'd finally admitted that he couldn't choose where his heart led him, he'd simply stopped fighting himself.

Although they could never have a future together, they had now. And he wasn't going to waste one more precious moment worrying about what he could not change. Whether they made love or not, he couldn't protect his heart from their eventual parting, so why not live life to the fullest while he was here and with her?

He'd never met a woman so strong. He knew what it took for her to yield to him. To give up her will, to allow him to do what he wished took such trust, faith and courage that he vowed not to disappoint her.

He'd washed his hands before he'd opened the door for room service, but he dipped his hands into the warm water of the finger bowl anyway, just for the sheer pleasure of using her shoulders and back to dry the back of his hands, saving her breasts for his palms.

Eyes wide, she licked her bottom lip, obviously enjoying his touch as much as he enjoyed caressing her. But his intention was to give them a cooling-off time and he turned to the cart of food. "Your throat must be parched. Would you care for a grape?"

"Yes, please."

He picked up the grape and placed it between her lips. As she brought it into her mouth and chewed, her eyes lit with simple enjoyment. He barely waited for her to swallow before he slanted his mouth over hers.

She immediately parted her lips, welcoming him into her sweetness. And he feasted, breathing in the citrus fragrance of her skin, tasting the fruit of the grape, sealing their bargain with a searing kiss that made him forget about food.

As his arms embraced her and drew her closer, he shut down the raw thought that whether or not he completed his mission, he couldn't keep her. The time bubble would collapse and send him back to the future. He could only have now.

So he vowed to remember every detail to take back with him to the future. Her kiss caused his emotions to swell into a tide of longing. He intended to ensure that today was a day she would never forget, one that would keep the lonely nights at bay, one that she'd look back upon through the years as the best of the best. If he could give her that, then he would have done his all.

He couldn't change the past, couldn't risk the future, but that didn't mean their time together was doomed. Today they would have more loving than many people had over the course of an entire lifetime.

He fed her tidbit after tidbit, whatever she wanted, taking care to let her swallow before he claimed another kiss. Then another. Between sizzling kisses, they sipped wine from the same glass and nibbled on treats that he fed her, each of them knowing the time was approaching when he was going to demand more from her.

So many ideas zinged through his head, so many choices. He wanted to do everything with her. But he went straight for the dessert.

He released her invisible bonds so she could once again move. When she noticed her new freedom, her eyes widened in surprise but she didn't change position. The pulse in her neck throbbed, indicating her recognition that her circumstances might be about to alter.

Bending forward, he kissed her again and at the same time skimmed his fingers along the insides of her thighs. She welcomed his kiss, leaning into his hands, which he grazed over her pubic hair. And when he gave that hair a tiny tug, her mouth opened wider, signalling her willingness for whatever he had in mind.

With featherlight caresses, he explored her shaved mons, shifting the chain slightly. As sensations rippled over her flesh, he enjoyed the twitches that revealed her eagerness for more. Gently, he peeled open her golden lips, still kissing her as he stroked and caressed. She responded with sweet moisture and as he dipped his fingers into her, he sensed her muscles quickening.

He'd denied her an orgasm earlier, making her wait, knowing that each time he raised the plateau to a new level, he increased the chance that the next time he wouldn't stop in time. Yet, her eyes and breath made it easy for him to tell when she was close to release. She wasn't deceptive by nature and during love play, she left not only her body open to him, but her emotions.

So as her legs gripped his and her fingers clutched her thighs, her breath came faster. He moved his fingers more quickly, taking her up hard and fast. And when he sensed that the next moment might be the one to take her over the edge, he stopped.

Her hips pumped asking for more. Her eyes widened in shocked surprise, but she didn't protest.

He gave her only a few moments to collect herself before he cupped her breasts and tweaked her nipples. Closing her eyes, she let out a soft groan. "Do you have any idea…how difficult it's become to let you do this?"

He had no intention of admitting he was having the same difficulty. Teasing her was causing his blood to riot and every drop seemed to have gone south. He ached to have her, with a desperate intensity. Desperation made some men weak. Kane prided himself on using that desperation to feed his determination.

Sweat beaded on his brow. Touching her breasts, watching the desire take over her expression and feeling her tremble beneath his hands fed his will. He was going to take her to places she'd never been before.

He had the skill. And somehow, somewhere, he would find the patience.

FALLON DIDN'T UNDERSTAND why he kept denying her release. He'd activated the buffs and with the combination of their vibrating pulsations, the snagging chain and his hands and mouth, she could think of little besides her flesh, her need and the indescribable sweet torture of being at his mercy.

She couldn't decide which was worse, being free to move but having to hold still, or being unable to move at all. Either way, she was always waiting, hoping he'd apply enough pressure in the right place to give her what she sought.

But he was a master at reading her. Although she

tried to hide how close she was to release, he always seemed to know.

"What do you like best?" he asked in lazy satisfaction. He tweaked her nipples. "This?" He slipped his hand between her legs. "Or this?"

"I like it best…when you…let me…come."

He continued to caress her intimately while he challenged her. "And suppose I don't let you come?"

She eyed him without the least bit of concern. "You won't do that."

"How can you be so certain?"

"Because you aren't cruel."

"Isn't making you wait cruel?"

"No." She shook her head. "Yes. Maybe." Talking while he stroked her was almost impossible, but she suddenly realized that it distracted her and allowed him to increase her pleasure without going over the top.

He laughed. "You've been very patient and now you'll receive a reward."

Her heart somersaulted. Finally, he was going to give her the orgasm she'd wanted for so long.

But instead of increasing the tempo, he withdrew his hands from her skin. Disappointment battled with uncertainty. Now what?

He swiveled the chair away from the desk, his eyes giving away nothing. She didn't have a clue what her reward was going to be. But when he set her on her shaking legs, it took more effort than she'd have thought just to stand.

He stood, too. And to ease the mounting tension,

she swallowed hard, very aware that he remained fully dressed while she always seemed to be naked. However, she didn't mind, not when he looked at her with such banked heat in his eyes. Just imagining unleashing all that fire warmed her.

"You will undress me."

He'd stated her reward as a command but she didn't care. She could have done a happy dance around the room but that would have delayed touching him. It seemed as if she'd been waiting forever to test the texture of his skin, bury her fingers in his hair, breathe in his scent.

Remembering how he'd made her clothing disappear with one tug, she fingered his shirt. "I want to take these off the way we do in our time."

"Whatever." His tone might have been casual but his eyes narrowed.

He'd figure out her plan soon enough. He'd spent hours driving her wild, teasing and taunting her, and now he'd actually commanded her to take off his clothes. And she fully intended to obey his demand—but she would do so her way.

Unless he objected, of course. But she didn't think he would from the glint of expectation in his gaze. Especially when she fingered the top button of his shirt, cocked her head and murmured, "It might take a while."

"I thought you were in a rush."

"That was before."

"Before?"

"Before you made my hands tremble."

He raised his hand to hers. "If you require my assistance—"

"I don't." She didn't even try to hold back her grin as she stroked his neck and ever so slowly traced a path down to the top button by his throat. "I can do this. And it's my reward, right?"

"Right."

He sounded just as sure of himself as he always did, when she finally unfastened the button and stroked the tiny vee of firm flesh that she'd just revealed. Although her anticipation had been building all day, she tamped down her eagerness, fully intending to use his own strategy against him.

However, as she leaned in to unfasten the next button, allowing her breast to brush against his shirt, she was very aware that he could put a stop to her teasing anytime he wished. Since he hadn't displayed one vulnerable moment—if she didn't count his admission of having once fallen in love—she expected him to be able to take quite a bit of her taunting before he decided her reward was done.

Wanting to throw him off balance, she unfastened the next four buttons quickly, yanked the tails from his slacks and then pulled the material over his shoulders, revealing his powerful chest. More like an Olympic swimmer than a weight lifter, his muscles were long and lean, his shoulders broad, his black chest hair tantalizingly soft. She threaded her fingers through the hair and ran her palms over his warm skin. Bronzed, muscular and firm, his chest tapered to a flat stomach.

She'd ignored his nipples but was pleased when her touch elsewhere caused them to tighten. Pretending to be unaware of the bulge in his slacks, she tipped back her head and skimmed her hands up and around his neck and into his hair. Silky and thicker than she'd expected, she tugged, drawing his head back a little, then lightly licked first one nipple, then the other.

"I'm enjoying my reward." She breathed the words onto his damp skin and watched him tighten further. She'd longed to touch him for so long that now that she could actually do so, the moment seemed magical. She wanted to give back every ounce of pleasure he'd given her, but she also wanted to see if she could reach him on more than a physical level.

Sure, they were playing sexual games—and mental games—but there was an emotional risk as well. Even if they could never be together again, she wanted evidence that her growing attachment to him was mutual. She wanted him as taut and tense and ready as she was. She wanted him to need with the same ferocity she did. And even if waiting delayed her own gratification, she still wanted to dig out an emotional response from him as well as a physical one.

She wasn't certain how she'd recognize whether or not she'd accomplished her goal, but proceeded with the certainty that he'd give her a sign so she'd know she'd succeeded. Perhaps his eyes would glimmer with a light she had yet to see. Perhaps his mouth would relax into an unguarded smile. Or perhaps she'd fail. She only knew that she had to try and reach him in a place that was elemental and raw.

She walked behind him and tugged the shirt over his shoulders, then flung it onto the desk. Technically, she was about to do more than disrobe him but she didn't expect him to stop her. She arched her spine and gently swirled her breasts against him. At the same time, she placed her arms around his waist and let her fingers drift over his tight abs and tense pectorals. When she tweaked his nipples as he'd done to her, he let out a slight hiss of air.

Pleased he hadn't stopped her, she pushed him further, using her hands and her breasts and nipping his back lightly. "So you like it when I touch you?"

"Of course. I'm not made of stone."

He sounded disgruntled, but marginally so, and she suspected he was giving in to not just the pleasure but his emotions, despite every intention not to. "I'm so glad you aren't stone. Stone is cold. Your flesh is warm and supple and pleasing."

"I'm glad you approve."

She grinned. "You don't sound glad. You sound… impatient."

"Wrong."

She disagreed. "In that case, you won't mind if I take my time to explore all of you?"

A muscle in the cords of his neck tightened. "Mind? Why would I mind?"

He was toying with her. Daring her. Challenging her. Telling her one thing with words, his body saying another. And she'd never been one to back down. Knowing that he found her touch arousing but refused to admit it caused a delicious thrill to spike. That he was fighting himself, and her too, told her that she could win this battle of wills. His emotions were buried deep, but he'd given her the means to dig them out.

But she would go slowly, sifting layer by layer until she discovered what was hidden at his core. She pressed her chest to his back, enjoying the ripple of tension that drew him ramrod straight. Touching him like this was causing her hands to tingle as if the friction was heating her palms and the blood in her veins.

Turning her head, she pillowed her cheek on his back, and allowed her hands to drop to caress his sex, which pushed against his slacks. At her touch through the material, he jerked. As her fingers scouted out the new territory, she imagined he wanted his clothes off as much as she wanted to take them off.

She adored how his flesh strained, marveled how he held himself in check. She wanted him to come unglued. But recalling how he'd made her wait and how the anticipation had intensified, she went slowly and listened as his previously even breathing altered to an occasional hitch. Oh, yeah. She figured he was due for some major caressing, especially after all he'd put her through.

She teased his length and when his legs stiffened rock hard, she sensed it was time to withdraw, but didn't let on to her disappointment. There were other ways to enjoy this gorgeous man. She walked around him and frowned at his now bulging zipper. "I need to take these off without doing any damage."

He didn't so much as bat an eyelash at her insinuation that she might accidentally injure his sensitive region. "I'm sure you'll manage."

She unfastened the top button, her fingers dipping into the waistband and skimming the head of his sex. Yum. No underwear. The idea of his tender flesh engorged just for her pleasure made her mouth water and her nerves hum.

Again he sucked in air between his teeth, half gasping, half gulping. "I could simply make my clothing vanish."

"But what would be the fun in that?" she countered, her tone playful.

She raised her eyes to take in his expression and found him watching her with an intensity that stole her breath. His dark blue eyes smoked and yet he still maintained complete control. She could see that the effort cost him in the hard set of his jaw.

But obviously, she hadn't pushed him far enough. Yet. Given enough time, she was certain she could shred his veneer of control.

She knew he was expecting her to slowly tease off his slacks but she wanted them off in one fast tug. Since he wore no underwear, she truly had to take care not to catch sensitive flesh on a zipper. So she compromised. She unfastened, unzipped and parted the material. When his straining sex sprang free, she sank her fingers into the wiry curls at the base. Carefully, she used her nails and tugged on the hair a little to put him on notice that she might not always be this gentle. And then she yanked down his pants.

Finally.

Finally he was as naked as she. Finally she was free to explore every delectable inch. And oh man did he have great skin—all bronzed and evenly muscled and in perfect proportions. She wasn't certain where she wanted to start first. Let him wonder for a change what she would do.

Fallon moved in slowly and cupped his balls, holding the heavy package in both hands. She was going to tease him as he'd done to her, using her hands and her mouth. And she was happily contemplating exploring his sexy bottom when she suddenly found she was no longer standing.

She was floating on air. Apparently he'd activated his antigravity mechanism, levitating her until she released her hold of him and their mouths were now at the same height. She was about to protest that he'd cut short her reward when he kissed her with a startling ferocity.

She responded without hesitation. Opening her mouth, her legs—and her heart. If he'd kept his perfect control, she would have been disappointed. The fact that he couldn't wait to make love to her pleased her, and the hard shell that had been softening around her heart melted.

Throwing her arms around his neck and locking her ankles around his hips, she took him inside her. With her floating, she didn't need him to help support her weight. His hands were free and one immediately found her clit, the other her bottom. And the delicate chain suddenly seemed to go berserk with their vibrating as he entered her and withdrew.

"Oh…you…feel good," he told her, his voice ragged and smoky.

"Mmm. You, too."

He felt better than good. With him filling her, his hands teasing her, the chain vibrating all her sensitive places, her need spiked so hard and so fast she couldn't breathe. And as his hips pumped into her, she met him stroke for stroke.

This was no sweet, take-your-time loving. This was all out thrusting and pumping. Her heart raced. Her breaths came in gasps. And when she exploded she couldn't hold back the scream as wave after wave crested and broke. Vaguely, she was aware he hadn't come with her. Vaguely, she was aware that his fingers never stopped dancing over her clit. Vaguely, she was aware that one orgasm rolled right into the next until she couldn't tell where one stopped and the next began.

And when she couldn't take any more, when she was certain he'd wrung her dry, he gave her another and then another until her body shook with electric pleasure. Her toes curled. The roof of her mouth went numb. She couldn't move, couldn't think.

And then he was clutching her bottom, pumping harder, faster, deeper. When he buried his mouth in her neck to muffle his hoarse shout of release, she drew him closer into her arms.

When she could once again speak, she didn't know what to say. She'd never realized she could experience such passion. And the knowledge that she'd never responded to any man like this, had never even realized she could, made her uneasy—until she reminded herself that this man was only in her life temporarily.

_10_

FALLON HAD SET herself up for heartache. But she'd become involved with Kane knowing he would leave and she didn't want to waste a moment worrying about future regrets. She'd have plenty of time for that later.

Right now, Kane was in her world, her time. Even as she contemplated using all the days they had left for making love, she knew his mission came first. So after they'd slept, showered and eaten breakfast, she understood that they had to go after Nigel.

Kane held out a pair of e-tickets. "We'll take a cab to Newark airport and fly to Las Vegas. I've already made the arrangements."

"Why not transport straight to Vegas?" she asked.

Already spoiled from his technology, she loathed the idea of wasting hours going through security, then flying. His kind of travel was instantaneous and the advantages of the saved time and convenience were addictive.

His tone was serious and determined. "I want Nigel to believe we're still in New York."

"And if we pop straight to Vegas, he'll know we're following him?" she guessed.

Kane nodded. "I need to catch him soon. He's slippery and sly and very intelligent."

No doubt he considered it a failure that Nigel had escaped him in New York. He hadn't complained but she suspected it bothered him. Fallon didn't mind so much. The longer Kane took to catch Nigel, the longer he would stay with her. However, even if he didn't catch Nigel, his time here was short. The time bubble had shrunk so that she needed to remain within ten yards of Kane or the illness returned.

Fallon didn't chafe at her restrictions. She liked being with Kane. However, she needed clothing. While he'd dressed himself, she was still wearing only gold dust and the fine chain. Since he hadn't shown her how to adjust the technology, she'd assumed he would clothe her as he had the day of the auction.

But as he headed for the door, she realized he must have forgotten. "Kane?"

"Yes?" He started to open the door to their suite.

"I'm not dressed."

"You look good to me." His eyes twinkled as his gaze raked her from bare breasts to shaved mons, his searing look shooting a shiver of desire to her core.

"And I'd be happy to be nude for you…in private."

"Why not in public?"

Her lower jaw dropped. He couldn't be serious. "Even if I was willing…I'd be arrested."

"Why?"

"We have laws against indecent exposure." She

frowned at him. He usually wasn't so unreasonable or so stubborn. She didn't mind his games; in fact, she enjoyed them. But she wasn't going to parade nude through the hotel and onto the streets of New York City.

"There's nothing indecent about nudity." He was teasing her, but she sensed a determination in him that made her nerves go raw.

She fisted her hands on her hips, but from his widening grin, she realized he wasn't taking her seriously. She hardened her tone. "I may be willing to do a lot of things for you, but going to jail isn't one of them."

He turned and advanced on her, gently placed his hands on her shoulders and urged her in front of a mirror. She took one look at her reflection. She should have known. In the mirror, she appeared to be wearing a cream blouse, navy jacket and matching skirt, with hose and leather pumps. But when she looked down at herself, she was naked.

"Amazing." She couldn't suppress a tremor of excitement as she realized he meant for her to parade around in public, naked to him, but fully clothed to everyone else. And she didn't think she could do it. The notion upset her in so many aspects that her mind was spinning. She'd pulled it off with Sinclair, but he'd been intoxicated, and she'd known him. She'd also been wearing a nightgown.

Kane didn't back down an inch but seemed to understand she required an explanation. "The technology isn't important. All you need to know is that

you won't be cold and your flesh will be as pro-
tected as if material surrounded you."

"If I step in a puddle?"

"Your feet won't get wet."

"And if I sit—"

"You skin will be safeguarded against germs, heat
or cold and the prying eyes of strangers."

He wanted her to walk around the city.

Naked.

He wanted her to pass right in front of strangers.

Naked.

He wanted her to take public transportation across
the country.

Naked.

She couldn't quite imagine such a thing. And she
feared that somehow he was fooling her. Like the
emperor in the story.

"I'm not sure I want to—"

"I want you to." His eyes pierced her and his lips
twisted in that knowing smile.

"But—"

"I'm not giving you a choice."

Oh…God.

"No one will see you but me." He'd told her he
wasn't giving her a choice, but his tone was coaxing
and gentle.

She licked her bottom lip to still the trembling.
"Suppose your technology fails?"

"It won't."

"You can't know that."

She reminded herself that she wasn't making a

spectacle of herself; everyone else would think she was dressed. Still, she needed to reevaluate. Was he going too far this time? Or was he simply pushing her out of her comfort zone? However, giving up more control to Kane when she felt most vulnerable somehow seemed right due to her growing feelings for him.

He took her hand and led her toward the door. She wondered what he'd do if she halted in her tracks and said *no*. Although she trembled, she couldn't deny the thread of excitement soaring through her panic. Going with him would be the most daring thing she'd ever done.

"Watching that chain tease you will help break up a boring plane trip."

"But—"

Her eyes jerked to his. Oh…my. The body buff had begun to tingle. And she'd already learned it turned on only when she wanted it to. So if she was becoming aroused, she obviously wasn't against his suggestion. But did that mean she didn't know her own mind?

As she squirmed and struggled with accepting that she was actually turned on, Kane laughed, an astute look in his deep blue eyes. "This is one trip you aren't ever going to forget."

Despite her shock and fears, excitement won out. And he knew it, damn him. She might not ever have found the nerve to step out of the suite, until he clasped her hand in his and tugged her.

In the hallway, a maid pushed a cleaning cart

down the hall. Fallon wanted to raise her hands to cover her breasts, but Kane kept a firm hold on one hand. And when the maid nodded a greeting but didn't so much as take a second look, Fallon was able to relax a little.

Waiting for the elevator was almost unbearable. Being naked in public—even if no one else could see her nudity—was nerve-racking. And giving up so much control to Kane had her questioning what in hell she was doing.

Her mouth was so dry, her voice came out a mere whisper. "This is the craziest thing I've ever done."

"And you look so beautiful when you blush." Kane teased, but his determination edged through. He was obviously taking way too much pleasure in her discomfort.

"So how come you aren't prancing around naked?" she muttered, annoyed that the delicate rings on her nipples were already making it hard for her to focus on their argument.

Kane laughed. "I wouldn't want to distract you."

She wanted to hit him. But she wanted to kiss him more. When the elevator opened and three people moved back to make room for them, she stiffened, half-expecting them to stare. But no one paid her the least bit of attention. And a look at herself in the mirrors reassured her that she appeared to be fully clothed.

Still, she found herself holding her breath as they exited the elevator, strolled through the lobby and then stepped through the double doors onto the busy city street. No one pointed at her. No one gasped. And when she forced her mind out of panic mode, she realized she wasn't the least bit cold. Nor did her feet feel as if they were touching the pavement. Instead, when she briefly closed her eyes, she felt as though the leather pumps really encased her feet and clothes swathed her body.

While Kane hailed a cab, she muttered, "This is so bizarre."

"You're doing fine."

A taxi pulled up to the curb. The idea of sitting naked on a dirty cab seat repulsed her. She opened her purse, floated a handkerchief over the seat before sitting.

"That's not necessary," Kane told her.

"Where to?" the cabbie asked.

Kane gave directions. The cabbie took off, making no comments about a naked lady in his backseat. However, the instant she relaxed, the body buffs noticed.

The buffs began to hum and vibrate. And no matter how many times she told herself she wasn't into parading around naked, the technology paid no attention.

That she'd apparently never known what she liked or wanted was infuriating. Especially because Kane seemed to know her better than she knew herself. Because now that she felt safe from exposure, she had to admit she was turned on by Kane's choice to keep her naked for his own enjoyment.

She might not appreciate that he'd given her no

choice, that he was pushing her out of her comfort area. But she could no more deny that she was aroused than she could that the sun rose in the east and set in the west. She liked Kane looking at her. Liked the way his eyes gleamed with pleasure. Liked the ironic twist of his lips that told her he'd known how she would react.

Even if she wasn't at ease, her elevated pulse and achy breasts told her that she was enjoying herself more than she should be. But who was to say this was wrong? She wasn't hurting anyone. She wasn't breaking any laws. Fallon could rationalize it from New York to Vegas, but the fact of the matter was that she found his desire to keep her aroused…erotic.

Still, when they arrived at the airport, her nerves drew taut again. She knew she was being silly. And she was torn. Because as much as she wanted her real clothes back, she had to admit she was thoroughly aware of her body in a way she'd never been before. She wasn't accustomed to seeing her breasts sway free with every breath, and when she exited the cab, she was oh-so-aware of the view Kane had of her bare bottom.

When her cell phone rang, she didn't want to answer it. She would rather think about Kane's reaction to her than problems at work. So she reached into her bag and then handed the phone to him.

And then it hit her. Kane was conditioning her. Even yesterday she might have answered her phone without thinking. But now…the outside world seemed like a big distraction. Was the technology altering her thought patterns? Or was it because she'd fallen for Kane and nothing else mattered? Either way, she was content to let him talk to Janet and confirm their hotel reservations in Vegas, content to let him make every arrangement.

Kane ended the phone connection and handed back her phone. "Nigel's still there."

"So what's the plan?" she asked. But she was really wondering what would happen when she went through airport security. Would his devices set off the alarms? What about the metal chain attached to every part of her? And what would happen if they asked her to remove her shoes? She gulped at the idea and her nerves racheted up another notch.

"We fly out to Vegas, check into the hotel and then I find Nigel."

"As soon as you catch him, you'll be going home?"

"Yes." His tone was easy but she'd learned to read him well enough to see the shadow of regret darken his eyes.

"And what about us?"

"There is no us. I'm sorry." His tone softened. "You've known that from the beginning. I must go back to my time. The laws of physics won't allow me to stay."

"Can you take me with you?" she asked, knowing it was unlikely. But his answer wouldn't change the fact that he'd come to care for her, too. He might not ever say the words or even admit them to himself. But his feelings came through to her, in the way his head lowered slightly and the way his bottom lips twisted to cover a grimace.

He shook his head, refusing to hold her gaze. "No one knows the answer to that question."

They passed by dozens of harried travelers. Men in business suits talking on cell phones and carrying laptops. Women pushing strollers with happy babies. Teens wearing tattoos and MP3 player headsets. No one paid her the slightest attention.

"What do you mean no one knows?"

"We've never brought anyone forward in time. It's too risky."

"Why? Won't the technology work?"

"It works."

"Then, why can't I go with you?"

"Because that would change the present and alter the future in ways we can't predict. You may be meant to have a child who grows up to be president, or you might develop a product that cures cancer."

"Can't history tell you whether or not my staying in this time is necessary?"

"If only it were that simple." They strode right through security with no problems and ambled toward their gate.

"I don't understand."

"For example, suppose next year you are in a car accident and someone's husband is killed. The wife remarries. If you leave with me, history will change. There's no accident, the wife doesn't remarry. Each of our millions of actions creates ripples in time that keep going. Just my being here with you for a few days may irrevocably alter the future. I could return home to a totally different time—especially if I don't catch Nigel."

Although he'd told her before that there was no possibility for them to remain together, she'd always hoped in the back of her mind that there might be a way out. Fallon wasn't the kind of woman to take no for an answer. She usually found a way to overcome most obstacles. But the scenario he presented her with was impossible.

She couldn't leave. He couldn't stay. And as much as she'd told herself she could handle the eventual separation, she knew it was going to be hard. So she welcomed the diversion of walking totally naked through the airport. And when the buffs and delicate chain tingled and teased her flesh, she accepted that she liked what the gadgets made her feel.

Would she like to spend her life in chains and naked? No. Would she want to give up her business and her search for a cancer cure forever? No. Did she want to stop talking to her family permanently? Of course not.

But the luxury of not having to worry about anyone but herself was a selfish indulgence that she wanted to last for as long as Kane was able to stay. She didn't want to miss a minute of their time together.

And when they boarded the plane and settled into the business class seats, she was sufficiently comfortable that she didn't bother placing her scarf between her and the seat. The technology was protecting her from curious eyes as well as germs.

So she relaxed and grinned at Kane. "Could we take our time chasing down Nigel?"

He leaned over and snapped on her seat belt, taking an opportunity to skim his hand over her belly and play with her chain, shooting direct heat between her legs. "What did you have in mind?"

"I know you made hotel reservations, but I have a house in Las Vegas."

He shook his head. "Sorry, I need to stay close to Nigel." Kane must have seen the disappointment on her face. "Don't worry. I'll make it up to you."

"How?"

He patted her hand. "You like surprises."

"No, I don't."

"You like *my* surprises."

She sighed and gave up. He wasn't going to tell her a thing. And she had to admit, so far his surprises had been right on target. He knew her desires and she trusted him. Although she had no idea what wild thing he might propose next, she'd decided to be open-minded. How could she not when he was so adept at giving her pleasure?

WHEN THEY FINALLY reached their Las Vegas hotel, Fallon took a shower. Kane consulted the television set. She wondered how he was able to communicate with his time through the television. Knowing he wouldn't answer her questions about the technology, she sank into a luxurious tub, turned on the jets and let the bubbling heat wash away the stress of traveling.

She felt a bit guilty for failing to check in with her family, but Janet had told them she was away on business, so they shouldn't be worried about her. Not that they ever were. Her family called when they needed something from her: advice, money, a shoulder to cry on.

Kane had taken her away from all that and she felt marvelously light. She hadn't realized how much caring for everyone had weighed her down until the load had been lifted. Janet would call if there was a true emergency, but otherwise Kane wouldn't put through the messages—which gave Fallon time to think about herself.

And about Kane.

She found it ironic that the first man who'd interested her in a long time, a man she cared for, was the one man she couldn't ever have. Leaning back her head on a rolled towel, she closed her eyes, appreciating the jets as they massaged away her aches. And she couldn't help wondering if the only reason she'd allowed herself to care about Kane was that there was no possibility of failure: he'd be gone long before she could screw up another relationship, as she had her marriage.

But she had to be fair. She was falling for him for many reasons. First, although he was very good at spending her money, her wealth was simply a means to complete his mission. Kane didn't desire the kind of life her money could buy—not only because he wasn't staying in her time, but material things as she knew them weren't important to him.

She'd never met a man more comfortable in his own skin. And while he was focused on his mission, he wasn't driven like a lot of high-powered men that she met who would be terrible husbands because they were already married to their jobs. Kane made time to talk and eat and make love.

She was immediately aware of him entering the bathroom. The bubble always made her sensitive to his proximity and she didn't have to open her eyes to know he was standing next to the tub, watching her, likely wondering if she'd fallen asleep. However, with the water tugging the delicate chain this way and that, sleep wasn't an option.

"You going to watch me or join me?" She opened her eyes, but her tone remained husky and lethargic, low and seductive.

"I wish I could." He fisted his hands on his hips. "You do look tempting."

"But?" she prodded.

"Nigel has been busy."

She sat up and frowned. "He's gone?"

Kane's eyes lowered and settled on her breasts. She told herself that her nipples hardened due to the cool air, but the truth was that his gaze alone could cause a physical reaction in her. Even worse, she'd gone all soft and fuzzy inside, making it difficult to follow the conversation.

Standing, she reached for a towel. But his hand closed on the thick terry cloth a second before hers. She glanced up to see his eyes bright with amusement and threaded with glittering blue heat. "I'll dry you."

"So what has Nigel done?"

"He's set up an exhibit of the technology he's offering for sale."

Kane folded a towel around her head to prevent her hair from dripping on the rest of her. Taking a second towel, he patted dry her forehead, her cheeks, her mouth. Seemingly in no rush, he made certain each area was dry before descending to her neck.

Meanwhile water droplets trickled over her, catching on the delicate chain. Although she attempted to remain still, she shivered and the buffs began to vibrate. One began to shave her mons. The other began to circle her right breast. But instead of distributing golden sparkles, this time the device decorated her with bold royal purple and silver glitter, leaving a swirling pattern that was both feminine and erotic.

She fervently wished the buffs were grooming her to make love, but she could tell from the tension in Kane's shoulders that they were going out. So she tried to ignore her disappointment, tried to ignore the body glitter, the towel skimming over her body and the delicious sensations that made her want to tackle him and make love.

Instead, she attempted to pretend she was unaffected. "An exhibit?"

"To sell his stolen gadgets, he must show potential buyers what they can do."

"We're going to try them out?" she guessed.

He shook his head. "We're going to see what kind of security he's set up. I wouldn't ask you to come with me, but—"

"If you leave me behind I'll be sick," she finished his sentence.

"Exactly. And since Nigel knows that I'm coming after him, he's going to be careful. He'll have a security system that will go off the moment it detects any technology from the future."

"What does that mean?"

"We can only bring items from your time with us. So we'll have to go shopping. For starters, we both need clothing. I'll need a weapon and if possible I'd like diagrams of the building."

"Ah, you're in my territory now." She picked up the phone. "May I?" Kane's eyes gleamed. He gave a sharp nod and she dialed the concierge. "This is Ms. Hanover. I'd like your shop to bring an assortment of men's and ladies' evening wear to my suite. Our luggage got lost so we'll need everything. Bring a variety of sizes." She hung up the phone pleased they wouldn't have to waste time shopping.

"What?" Kane teased. "You aren't going to purchase a weapon and plans over the phone?"

"That's something I can't do for you, but Logan Kincaid can." She handed him the phone.

"The Shey Group is not at my beck and call."

"So hire them. I can think of better things to do with our time."

11

KANE HIRED the Shey Group to get him detailed information on the building and the security specs he wanted. However, he couldn't let Fallon delay his plans for the evening with a bout of lovemaking. As much as he would have enjoyed holding her once again, kissing her and getting to know more about her likes and dislikes, Kane had business on his mind and wasn't about to allow her to distract him from his mission.

Fallon dressed in real clothes, with no buffs or chain attached to her body for the first time in days. She hadn't realized how accustomed she'd become to the gadgets, but the lack of the objects reminded her of the days after her divorce. She'd removed her wedding band, but her finger had felt bare. Now when she walked, she felt as though something was missing. Her breasts felt almost too light and she missed the tugging on her flesh that reminded her of their lovemaking.

"Aren't you worried that Nigel will recognize us?" she asked as they stepped into the empty elevator on the way down to the lobby.

Kane pushed the button to close the doors. "We have appointments in the salon. Will you like me as a blonde?"

She eyed him, her gaze narrowing. "Changing your hair or eye color isn't going to do it. Even if we could bleach your skin, your shoulders are so distinctive that—"

"There's a man downstairs who assured me that my own mother won't recognize me when he gets through with me."

"You've never mentioned your family before."

"The less you know about the future the better."

She frowned. "How can knowing about your relationship with your family alter anything?"

Kane sighed. "That's always the problem. You aren't even supposed to know that I'm here. Anything I say could—"

She rolled her eyes. "Oh—pul-lease. If you don't want to tell me about yourself, don't. But I'm not buying such ridiculous excuses."

The elevator doors opened and the sounds and sights of the casino kept their conversation private. Buzzers chimed as the slots paid out. A roulette wheel spun, people betting as the big wheel rolled. A woman at the craps table screamed and pumped her fists at a big win.

But they headed away from the gambling, toward the shops that catered to the big winners. He escorted her past a jewelry store and an art gallery to the salon. "I have two brothers and two sisters. I'm the oldest."

"And what do your parents think about your job?"

He shrugged. "Since Dad's a time cop and his father ran the Shey Group, my folks are accustomed to their children risking their lives for good causes."

"Your brothers and sisters—"

"It's the family business. I believe in this time, The Shey Group was limited to men, however that will change soon."

"Maybe I should join up?" She grinned at him. "After you leave, my life might seem rather dull. I could use—"

The intensity in his voice strengthened. "You can't change your life because of meeting me."

"So do you know what I do with the rest of my life?"

"I have no idea. If I'd known you were going to get caught in the time bubble, I would have thoroughly researched you before I left. But since our being together is a mistake—"

She lifted her eyebrow and allowed her pique to show. "Is that how you think of me? As a mistake?"

"You know what I mean. I will never regret our time together on a personal level. However, after I'm gone, you must continue as if I was never really here, as if I was a dream. If I could make you forget everything, I would."

"So you don't have a gadget to wipe memories clean?" she asked, keeping her voice low as they strolled past a boutique and a gift shop.

"We were working on it. But the brain is a strange organ and quite uncooperative when it comes to manipulation of memories. I believe our scientists have given up."

She sensed there was much more he wasn't saying because disapproval and relief came through as clearly as his words. Had scientists in the future experimented on people and damaged their minds? She had no idea and knew better than to ask because the grim look on Kane's face said he didn't like the direction the conversation had taken.

To lighten the moment, she teased, "So what do you think about purple hair to match the glitter on my breasts?"

"That would attract too much attention."

She pursed her lips. "So I'm going for the mousy librarian look?"

He bent and kissed her. "You could never be mousy. I was thinking you could get a wig, and then you wouldn't have to ruin your hair."

Pleased that he liked her the way she was, she nodded. "A wig and makeup won't be enough for you."

"The man on the phone told me he's done hair and makeup for films and has all kinds of tricks up his sleeves. Let's see what he can do."

Less than thirty minutes later, Fallon was wearing glasses, an auburn wig and lots of makeup. She was certain her family wouldn't recognize her, and when she saw Kane, she had to look twice, and then she stared. He was at least two inches taller and appeared to have gained fifty pounds. His shoulders no longer looked huge because of his padded belly.

Longish straggly hair fell around his shoulders. The pièce de resistance was the set of slightly buck teeth.

She chuckled. "My...aren't you attractive."

"Does the disguise work?" he asked, his tone worried. The teeth made him speak with a lisp.

"If I hadn't known it was you, I wouldn't have recognized you."

"Good." He didn't sound pleased. He still sounded as though Nigel was going to figure out their real identities.

"What's wrong?" she asked.

"I don't like bringing you into danger."

She shuddered at her memories of the nausea.

He threaded his arm through hers. "It's just that I'm not supposed to be here and neither are you. Putting you into danger is a huge risk. If there's trouble—"

"I am a trained CIA operative," she reminded him, wishing she hadn't had to leave behind her gun. But he'd feared that Nigel's security would spot it in a heartbeat and prevent them from entering the exhibit.

"Nigel's trained to fight and he's stronger than you. In fact, he's stronger than I am."

"Really?"

She'd seen Nigel and his muscles hadn't impressed her. He was shorter than Kane and must have weighed fifty pounds less. And since Kane was solid muscle behind all the padding of his disguise, she was having trouble believing what he'd just told her.

"Nigel's strength has been...enhanced."

"Through drugs?"

"It's new technology that can open his arteries and veins to pump more blood, oxygenate his muscles and contract them artificially. The technology gives him superhuman strength. But if he activates it, he'll pay afterward by suffering numbing fatigue."

"So he won't use it unless he must," she concluded. Fallon didn't like the fact that Nigel seemed to have everything in his favor. First, he had the home ground. They had to go to him and he obviously expected them to try something with all the security precautions he had in place. If she hadn't had the clout with the concierge to wrangle an invitation to the exhibition, they wouldn't have gotten inside. And they had to go in without their weapons, something that made her feel vulnerable. Then to learn Nigel had superhuman strength was a fact that Kane wouldn't have revealed unless he was worried.

Yet, Kane had no choice but to follow where Nigel led and she would do her best to help him. So she studied her fake identification, memorizing her new name and identity while Kane looked over the specs that the Shey Group had sent.

"When we get there, be very careful what you say." Kane tossed the specs onto the counter. "Nigel knows I'm coming after him. But he knows I always work alone and he may not be expecting a couple. I'm hoping he didn't realize we were together at the auction."

"How do you plan to catch him?"

"Tonight is simply our chance to check his operation and security. Until I see his setup and what he's selling, there is no plan."

She relaxed a little and threaded her arm through Kane's. They took the elevator to the penthouse suites where a man in a tuxedo and white gloves met them as the doors swished open. He gestured them forward, then held out his hand palm up. "Welcome. Invitation, identification and funds, please."

The invitation had cost Fallon a hundred thousand dollars. Apparently, Nigel wanted to keep out anyone who wasn't serious. And Fallon wasn't exactly certain what a look at the exhibit entailed, but the concierge had told her that the seller promised they wouldn't be disappointed.

"Everything is in order?" Kane asked Nigel's man, who didn't flinch at Kane's authoritative tone.

He calmly continued to examine their documents and when he leaned forward, Fallon saw the outline of a weapon holstered beneath his shoulder. Finally, he handed the documents back and placed the cashier's check in his front pocket. "If you will please follow me, I'll explain the procedures."

They walked down a hallway lined with an exquisite Oriental runner. Oil paintings hung on the wall and a jade fountain gurgled, the scent of floating white blossoms adding a cloying scent to the air.

"Your check buys you an evening to try the technology and ensure that it works as promised. If you desire, paid companions have been arranged to join you."

Kane slung an arm over her shoulder. "I have all the companionship I need with me."

"That's your prerogative, sir." The guard stopped in front of a set of double doors. "I will remain here for your protection."

More likely to prevent them from stealing the technology, Fallon thought as she strove to keep a bland expression on her face. With only the one entrance and exit, there would be no sneaking in or out. She would have to purchase the technology, again. And she was certain that Kane would not allow her to keep it. Although the waste of capital bothered her, she understood the stakes and accepted that she could well afford the loss.

But perhaps more importantly, she trusted Kane to do the right thing with her money. If he spent some of her wealth, it wasn't out of greed but for a higher purpose—one she admired as much as she admired him.

She'd loved before. Never easily, but she'd loved. Yet, oddly, she'd never trusted a man with her wealth—until now. And the idea was freeing. He was a man worthy of her love and her trust. And somehow just knowing that made her realize she'd finally gotten all that she'd ever wanted—even if she only had him for a while.

Nigel's man spoke carefully, as if he'd been required to memorize his message. "Further instructions are on the dining table. Please understand that once you exit the premises, you won't be allowed to return."

They strode inside and Fallon ignored the pleasant fragrance of flowers in vases and the spicy scent of cinnamon candles. She walked past a table covered with a delicate lace tablecloth and set with a tempting assortment of hors d'oeuvres and cheeses, a sterling ice bucket enticingly offering chilled Dom Perignon and chocolate-dipped strawberries. Instead, she let her gaze sweep around the room, noting the security cameras that seemed to cover every angle before making a beeline for the brochure on the dining room table.

She picked up the note and read aloud. "Welcome. Your check buys you the once-in-a-lifetime opportunity to try out the newest in pleasure technology. While the security is tight throughout the suite, the master bedroom and bath are private." She glanced at Kane, her curiosity engaged. What kind of device was he selling this time that it required the assurance of privacy in the master bedroom? "Do you think that's true?"

Kane shrugged and popped the cork on the champagne. "Does it really matter?"

"I don't want to end up on the Internet," she muttered, remembering her cover in case they were being audio-monitored. "Mother wouldn't like it." Then she went back to reading aloud. "After your opportunity to try my little invention, I'm certain you'll wish to submit a sealed bid. The winner will be notified the day after tomorrow and will be expected to transfer the funds immediately. At that time, all four prototypes, the patent pending and full legal documentation will be legally transferred. You are welcome to stay the night. Enjoy, and good luck with the bidding."

She frowned at the brochure and turned it over. The other side was blank.

"What's wrong?" Kane asked, smoothly pouring two flutes of champagne without wasting a drop.

"I still don't know why you dragged me here."

"Patience." He handed her a flute and leaned forward.

To the cameras, he'd appear to be nuzzling her ear, but he whispered. "Walk around the room."

She sipped her champagne, then ambled to the windows where she had a view of the Las Vegas strip. The numerous bright lights lit up the street like the sun and thousands of residents, tourists and convention-goers hurried down the huge sidewalks, seemingly eager to spend their money gambling.

"The view is lovely."

She glanced to Kane and noted that while he appeared to be watching her, his gaze slid past her right shoulder. "I'm a lucky man."

The surveillance equipment would simply show Kane complimenting her. Stalling to give Kane time to check the security, she played along. "If you play your cards right, you might get even luckier."

"Unless you're talking about strip poker, playing with cards isn't what I had in mind."

Although his banter was strictly for any listening devices, she couldn't help but heat up at his tone. He might have been working but the intensity behind his words was very real and pleasure shimmied through her. Being with Kane excited her on several levels. Their work was important and the fact that he'd shared information more than he should have with her meant that he trusted her. Also, she liked combining business and pleasure. And last but just as important, she liked the way he always tried to protect her, making her feel valuable and cherished.

Remembering his instructions to walk around, she strolled by the windows, detoured into the kitchen and opened and closed the fridge, then returned to the dining table and surveyed her choices. The decision between the chocolate-dipped strawberries and apricots was a tough one, but the strawberry called to her taste buds. Perhaps it was her nerves, perhaps because Kane was watching, but the fruity chocolate went down sweet and smooth.

She held up another strawberry. "Want to try one?"

"Oh, yeah."

Finally Kane seemed satisfied enough with his security preparation to join her. He dipped his head and she thought he meant to take the strawberry into his mouth or whisper into her ear, but he planted his lips on hers. "Mmm."

He might be on a mission, but he hadn't forgotten how to kiss—even with fake buck teeth. She never knew exactly what to expect from Kane. Sometimes he was exceptionally tender and gentle. Other times he was demanding. This time he kissed her as if he'd been craving her and his heat stoked her kindling embers until she forgot the cameras and who might be watching. His lips on hers became her sole focus. That and the fact that she wanted more.

And when his arms came around her, gathering her close, she couldn't think of one place she'd rather be. Compared to kissing Kane, the technology in the next room would seem dull.

The champagne on his lips intoxicated her and she wished that all their clothes and his padding weren't between them. But if his mouth was the only part of his body she could touch, she would take what he gave her. When they broke apart, her pulse had escalated and she had to breath in deeply for air.

And when he took her hand, she was ready to discover whatever was waiting for her in the master bedroom. If security cameras were watching them, they had to go and inspect the technology, even try it out or their actions would be highly suspicious.

While Kane surveyed the master bedroom with sharp eyes, she looked around. The suite appeared normal—high, sweeping ceilings and lots of marble, gilt and glass that one would expect in a penthouse suite. An exceptionally large bed dominated the room. Custom-made, the bed had to be almost double king-size and round. The rich emerald coverlet matched the drapes and dozens of pillows in assorted shapes and hues of green and gold drew her eye to a tiny scarlet velvet box that perched in their midst.

She was about to approach and examine the scarlet box when Kane tugged her back into his arms. Lifting her head, she hoped for another stunning kiss. But his fingers unfastened her blouse with an expertise that told her he was in a hurry and his knowing smile warned her that he knew exactly what was in the box.

She glanced at the ceiling. "What about cameras?"

"There aren't any in here."

He sounded so certain, but he wasn't a man to take another's word, especially one who worked for Nigel. She leaned forward, catching his fingers, and lowered her voice. "How do you know there aren't any hidden cameras or microphones?"

He waved a brochure that he must have picked up while she'd been taking in the ramifications of that awesome bed. "Because the device Nigel stole has built in privacy dampeners. You needn't worry about anyone hearing what you say or looking at all your delicious skin except me, and me, and me."

By now she knew Kane well enough to take his explanations on faith. Besides, he'd never jeopardize the mission by risking being caught,

She laughed at his odd turn of phrase. Most of the time they had no communication problems, either physical or verbal. He wasn't a man to hide what he wanted from her or from himself.

At the moment he seemed more concerned with removing her blouse than playing with the new toy waiting for them on the bed. And while his eyes glinted lasciviously, his touch was careful and precise.

He didn't tease her flesh as he parted the blouse and she shrugged it off. Yet, she'd learned that if she didn't undress him, he'd soon have her naked. While that was fine by her, both of them naked would be better.

So she removed his shirt and the padding with the same swift efficiency he'd used. And she couldn't help wondering if this was the last time they'd make love. He had a plan to catch Nigel and once he put it into effect, Kane would be out of her life—forever.

Knowing this could be goodbye made a lump well up in her throat. Kane had come to mean so much to her. No matter how lonely she became later, she would never regret this time with him. He'd taught her that she could be wanted for herself and for that, she would always hold a part of him tenderly in her heart.

She tossed the long strands of hair aside to reveal his true profile. She wanted to memorize the tiny crinkle lines by his eyes, the bold nose, the lips that so often twisted into an amused smile, lips that had kissed every part of her body and given her so much pleasure.

She didn't have so much of a photograph of him but she took a mental snapshot. His broad chest and wide shoulders thrilled her as much as the demanding expression now on his face, and her heart hitched as she wondered what he had in mind. By the flaring of his nostrils and the glimmer of light in his eyes, she could tell he was up to something…something delightfully wicked.

"What are you smiling about?" He reached to unfasten her slacks.

"I'm finding that I do like your surprises but…"

"But?"

"You have that cat-that-ate-the-canary look."

"Huh?"

Her wording might have confused him, but his hands never stopped removing her slacks. In no time she was standing there in an apricot lace bra and matching bikini panties.

"You look like you can barely wait to spring this next surprise on me."

He grinned and kicked off his shoes. "You are so correct. Take off all my clothes, please."

This was a switch. He got to be naked first. She didn't hesitate, removing his slacks, bending to take off his socks, all the while wondering what he was up to. If she hadn't been so on edge, she might have tried to tease him as she took off his clothing, but as he tensed in anticipation, she sensed he wanted to get past the removal of the clothing to the seduction.

Good.

For once their eagerness to make love seemed to be on the same wavelength. Kissing him had incited her hormones to riot. Undressing him had aroused her to a seven or eight on her readiness meter. Already, she wanted to ditch her bra and panties. In fact, when she straightened she expected him to do so in short order.

Naked and aroused, he gestured for her to join him by the bed. With a sparkle in his eyes, he picked up the scarlet box.

"What's in there?" She expected a sex toy. Special oils. An aphrodisiac. Perhaps a different version of the buffs or chain that she'd worn before.

"We're going to have fun and since Nigel would

be suspicious if we didn't spend the night, we might as well enjoy the technology."

He opened the box and she peered inside. Her eyes had trouble focusing. It looked like liquid diamonds all sparkling and mysterious. Was it something to drink?

Kane lifted the box over his head and turned it upside down. She thought the sparkles would drip over him, like thick honey. Instead, the substance unfurled like a ball of yarn, the sparkling thread winding over Kane's face, his neck, his chest, his stomach. It wound over his sex and buttocks, his legs, almost like a heavenly measuring tape with a mind of its own.

"What is it?" she asked.

"You'll see."

The tape shined and shimmied, filling in the gaps until not a sliver of his bronze flesh showed through the silvery diamond sparkles. Then the silver cracked and opened down the center and Kane stepped away. The material lacked his body to cling to but closed back on itself and nevertheless held his shape like a mold.

And then the silver threads vanished. Leaving behind an exact duplicate…of Kane.

"Oh, God." She looked from the duplicate to Kane. "There're two of you?"

Kane gestured to the silver thread that was busy duplicating him yet again.

"Actually, there're three of me now. All ready to pleasure you."

12

After Kane had heard the setup, the luxury suites, the private showing, the funds required to check out the technology, he'd suspected that Nigel was going to sell the Hot Copier, nanotechnology that replicated "Hard Copies" of sexual partners. Fallon may have already seen too much of the future technology but Kane figured that one more item wouldn't make too much difference in the grand scheme of time. Besides, Nigel would know if he didn't activate the Hot Copier, and that would be suspicious.

Kane grinned at the fact that, though sometimes working as a time cop was a difficult job, right now he couldn't have been more pleased. As he smiled, HC1 and HC2 smiled, too, replicating him down to his atomic base point.

Fallon gasped, her jaw dropping as her gaze flitted from HC1 to HC2 to Kane. "Are they real?"

"Sort of. Hard Copies have no past, no future. But when a Hard Copy touches you, you will feel him as you would me. Hard Copies can do everything I can do—my hands, my lips, my tongue."

Her gaze dropped to his erection.

Kane chuckled. "That too."

"This is…impossible." She took a step toward HC1, her breasts deliciously quivering in the lacy bra.

"In your time, it isn't possible," he agreed, enjoying her curiosity as she strode around the Hard Copies, giving him an opportunity to admire her long legs, her rounded bottom and her trim waist. He loved keeping her naked. If he had his way he'd keep her nude all the time. But Nigel would have detected the technology. However, now that she was almost bare again, he smiled a grin of satisfaction.

"These guys are outrageous."

"You like outrageous," he reminded her, thoroughly enjoying himself and knowing it was simply a matter of time until she gave in and accepted what would please her.

"But I'm not into sexual toys."

"Hard Copies aren't mere mechanical toys."

"Really?" She ran an experimental finger down HC1's arm, then leaned in and sniffed. "He smells just like you."

"He also thinks exactly as I direct him to."

Her eyes widened and she took a step back. "These…"

"Hard Copies," he supplied the word for her, and despite her shock the name made her lips quirk in amusement.

"These Hard Copies have a brain?"

"Enough to obey my commands."

Her gaze darted to him. "You control them?"

"Yes." He enjoyed watching her take in the concept, trying to think through the ramifications. Although he couldn't answer more than basic questions she might have about the technology, since he wasn't a nanotechnologist, he could see what she knew already was stirring her excitement.

"How many of these Hard Copies can one…" With a frown, she gestured to the scarlet case where the liquid nanobots had returned by themselves.

"The device is called a Hot Copier."

She laughed, her lips wide and full, and shook her head, spilling a lock of hair over one her eye. "So how many Hard Copies can a Hot Copier make?"

He folded his arms over his chest and directed HC1 and HC2 to do the same by shooting a thought command their way. "You don't think three of us are enough to satisfy you?"

She didn't hesitate, cocking one brazen hip in his direction. "You are enough all by yourself."

"Ah, but think of three sets of hands on you simultaneously exploring. Three sets of lips tasting."

"This is…insane."

"You like insane."

She ignored his comment as though disagreeing but her hardened nipples poking through her apricot bra told a different story. Oh, she was excited all right—perhaps a little reluctant to admit it, but he was now certain he could overcome any twenty-first century hesitation.

"So how do you tell them what to do?" she asked, her curiosity clearly intense.

"I think at them."

"And they won't do anything—"

"Nothing, unless I instruct them."

She swallowed hard, her flat belly shimmying in a delightfully erotic movement and he saw that a spark of interest joined the curiosity in her expression. "So these Hard Copies are like a computer that you program by thought?"

"You can think of them that way."

He stepped forward and tugged her into his arms, loving the softness of her skin, appreciating the way her tense muscles relaxed on contact with his, then trembled in eager anticipation. Oh, she was quite a woman, Fallon Hanover. Since his arrival, she'd absorbed one surprise after another, and now he would enjoy giving her more pleasure than she'd ever believed possible. It was the least he could do after disrupting her life, dragging her on a dangerous mission and then allowing them to grow close.

He'd known from the start of his mission that he would have to leave her behind. He'd been through that painful experience once, but his feelings had never before been this strong. And each time they made love, every day that passed, intensified his growing feelings.

Damn it. He'd told himself not to repeat his mistakes. But how could he fail to cherish her when she was so open to new ideas, to adapting to new challenges, to accepting him? As he kissed her and she kissed him back, he realized he might have found the perfect woman—and he couldn't keep her.

Pain lanced deep but he did his best to set it aside. Tonight was for them to enjoy. Tonight he would make unforgettable. Tonight he would create enough precious memories to last a lifetime.

He waited until she wrapped her hands around his neck, and then he instructed HC1 to nibble one of her delectable ears and HC2 the other. He needed merely to think about teasing her sensitive lobes with his lips and the Hard Copies would follow through.

Although she'd had warning, at the first nip to her ears she broke her kiss with him. The Hard Copies kept right on nibbling, per his orders, and he tugged her back for another kiss. He didn't think she'd resist, but he didn't quite expect her to sigh so contentedly, either.

"You do know how to make me happy, don't you?" She kissed his nose, his chin, his jaw. "What I don't understand is how you know what I want better than I do."

"It's because I'm brilliant."

"And sensitive."

"Of course."

"And the world's greatest lover."

"If you insist."

"And so humble, too," she teased.

"You wouldn't adore humble," he teased right back.

Her eyes gleamed with challenge and a bold sauciness that he'd come to appreciate. "Who says I adore you?"

"You didn't have to say so. I can tell by the way you react to me."

"So now you can read my mind, too?"

"Oh, yeah." The Hard Copies nibbled her shoulders and, eyes sparkling, she quivered. He lowered his hands to her bra and unsnapped the clasp at the back. "You like lots of attention. You'll like it even better when we worship your flesh with our tongues."

Each Hard Copy slid a shoulder strap down onto her arm. She was about to shrug off her bra when he stopped her with a curt demand. "Do not move."

"Or else…?" she prodded, her eyebrow raising in speculation.

"Or else I'll take twice as long," he threatened, watching her irises darken with hungry comprehension. "That's right. You're going to stay still and do exactly as I say, when I say it."

"Yes."

"Or you will suffer the consequences." He saw her lips twitch in delight. Oh yeah. Fallon loved to play games. She liked it when he took charge and freed her to simply enjoy what he had to give. And he and the Hard Copies could give more than she'd ever imagined.

"Think of HC1 and HC2 as extensions of me."

"Okay." She licked her bottom lip and stood straighter, her breasts swelling beneath the lace and causing the fabric to slide until one shrug would free them.

Kane wanted her so much that holding back wouldn't be easy. Yet, for her he was determined to do whatever he must to give her a night she would never forget. It wouldn't be fair to tell her how much she meant to him, not when they would live the rest of their lives separated by more than a century. While he couldn't tell her with words, he could show her with actions. He intended to savor every moment, cherish her, adore her, because the time bubble was collapsing and their time together running out.

FALLON'S AMAZEMENT over the Hard Copies quickly switched to excitement. It didn't matter that she hadn't a clue how the Hard Copies worked. She didn't understand the engine in her car but that didn't stop her from driving it. So the scientific principles behind the Hard Copies didn't matter. Kane had explained the important points. He was in charge. The Hard Copies followed his thoughts. So, as he'd instructed, she thought of the replicas as an extension of Kane. Instead of using a feather to stroke her skin, he'd employed the Hard Copies to nibble along her neck.

And if she'd had any doubts about who was in control, the way Kane put his knowledge about her body to use dispersed those doubts. Just as Kane knew where and how she liked to be touched, so did HC1 and HC2. They homed in on the sensitive spot behind her ear and another at her neck with total accuracy.

Her bra now hung from her nipples. One deep breath would free her straining flesh. And she oh-so-wanted to be as naked as Kane.

When he angled his mouth over hers for another

kiss, she had to stiffen her legs to prevent leaning into him. But then at the same time as Kane's kiss, the Hard Copies each took a nipple into their mouths right through the lace material and she forgot all about standing still.

She gasped into Kane's mouth and flung her arms around him for balance but ended up embracing each of the Hard Copies instead, men who felt exactly like Kane. Stunned by the sensory overload, she quivered and clung to HC1 and HC2 as they continued to swirl their mouths over her captured nipples.

Her belly swooped at the dual tugs. But it was the fire in Kane's eyes that made her breath catch. She had no idea what he intended to do to her, but her anticipation upped another notch.

Tongues lapped through the lacy material and it took concentration to not only follow the conversation but to keep her thoughts from moving ahead. They had the entire night in this suite and had only been here less than thirty minutes. Yet, she was already aching for an orgasm. The tiny strip of lace between her legs was damp with moisture.

And then Kane dived down and took her mouth in a fiercely possessive kiss, his hands tipping up her chin. Meanwhile the Hard Copies' hands caressed her breasts, her belly, her thighs. Three mouths, three pairs of hands, all stimulating and simultaneously giving her pleasure.

No one could have stayed still under such conditions. No one. Her body shivered and gyrated to the rhythm of the caresses.

Kane broke the kiss and directed the Hard Copies to release her. He pointed to a drapery tie. "Since
you cannot hold still. I will bind you. Bring me the
ties."

When she turned to obey, her bra fell from her
breasts and slipped to the floor. Good riddance. She
hurried to the drapery ties, remembering the last time
he'd kept her still with the buffs and the chain. But
she no longer wore those so he was devising a new
plan.

It had been difficult enough to bear the intense
pleasure Kane alone gave her. With him directing the
Hard Copies, she knew she was about to undergo a
wondrous experience. And yet, her mouth was dry.
The idea of being so helpless and vulnerable rock-
eted up her nerves to almost unendurable levels.

She unfastened the drapery tie and turned to bring
it to him, hoping the man in the center of the identical triplets was the real Kane. She handed him the
drapery cord as if she had no doubts but was unable
to control the telltale trembling in her hands.

"You'll require more than one."

She nodded and went back to gather the others.
The idea of being helpless while all those hands and
mouths roved over her exposed flesh thrilled and
tormented her, and made every step back to Kane
seem to take forever.

"The Hard Copies will remove your panties." At
his command, both of them kneeled and in unison
peeled down her panties with their teeth. And their
lips seared a blazing trail down her sides while their

hands lightly skimmed her buttocks and thighs as if giving gentle promise of what was to come.

Kane tugged off the coverlet to expose forest-green sheets. "You will lie there." He pointed to the middle of the bed, his gaze evaluating the bed frame that curved completely around the bed's perimeter. And for the first time she noted the upright bed posts, which would allow him to bind her however he pleased.

She sat on the bed and scooted backward. Kane ambled around and stopped at a point above her head. "Cross your wrists and place your arms over your head."

She did as he asked, surprised at how swiftly and tightly he wrapped her wrists without hurting her. With one end around her wrists he tied the other to the bed frame, but didn't pull too tightly, leaving her arms comfortably bent above her head.

While Kane tied her wrists, HC1 and HC2 tied her ankles, spreading her legs, but leaving enough slack for her to bend her knees if she liked. Feeling totally exposed, her heart sped in anticipation as she waited for them to join her.

So Kane shocked her when he and the Hard Copies turned to leave the room. She lifted her head, startled and upset. "Where are you going?"

"Will you miss us?" Kane asked.

"Yes." Of course she would miss him. How dare he promise her all kinds of pleasure and then walk away.

"Good." He shot her one of those arrogant looks

that told her his mind was set and nothing she could say would change it. And as he stared between her legs with satisfaction, arousing her with just a look, she knew she'd met her match. She might be furious at his game. She might not want to wait. But every moment would be sweet torture. Every moment she spent thinking about what he was going to do would feed her arousal.

Impatience made her come close to begging. "Kane, I already want you."

"Close your eyes," he demanded.

"But—"

"Close them or I'll blindfold you."

She snapped her eyes shut, totally irritated, totally frustrated, completely aroused. It wasn't fair that he could look at her and he wouldn't let her do the same. And now she wouldn't know when he returned. She'd jump at every sound, twitch at every breath of air-conditioning.

She heard footsteps coming toward her and held her breath. Maybe she'd changed his mind. But then she felt him tying a scarf around her eyes.

"What are you doing? I didn't look."

"And now you can't."

She groaned. "Don't you trust me to keep my word?"

"Now you don't have to fight with yourself. You have absolutely nothing to do except think about how much pleasure I'm going to give you."

Every cell in her sparked.

"Ah, Fallon, Fallon, Fallon." His voice swept over

her like a silken caress. "Your body is so adorable. Your breasts are exquisite. Your sweet crease is already filling with moist honey and the scent is driving me wild."

Fallon sucked in her breath. Sweat broke out on her forehead and she twisted against her bindings. She couldn't see. Couldn't move.

Suddenly, an icy bead of fluid dropped between her legs. At the cold, she jerked. "Kane?"

He didn't answer.

But he was there. She tensed. Icy drops spatted on her nipples, dribbled over her breasts. And then three mouths closed on the cold with fiery heat. With a mouth on each nipple and one between her legs, every muscle in her body tensed in expectation of more cold.

"Is it champagne?" she asked.

"Yes," was his curt reply.

Then with no warning, warm hands soothed a fragrant oil over her shoulders and neck, her belly and thighs, her arms and feet. Six hands caressed and stroked, moving as one, moving in unison, and as the oil heated her flesh, she began to tug against her bonds.

She wanted to touch. She wanted to see. She wanted to reach out and draw Kane against her singing flesh.

But the tight bonds kept her exactly where he wanted her to be. And then once again, the icy cold droplets pricked at her nipples and mons and she tensed, praying his mouth would return too and warm her. She didn't know how, but she was certain Kane's was the breath blowing between her legs. And when the heat followed the cold, she lifted her hips into him, wanting more of his magical mouth. His hands slipped under her bottom, holding her to him.

He ran his tongue over first the outside of her lips, then delved to the inside. As scrumptious as he felt, he ignored her sweet spot where she wanted him most. And as he directed the Hard Copies' mouths over her breasts, she realized he was deliberately keeping her from going over the edge. She needed more, harder, faster.

Kane gave her slow, sensual, seductive.

And as her slick flesh became more slippery, he increased the tempo, as did the Hard Copies, but never quite enough. And between the hands and the lips, every inch of flesh on her body received simultaneous caresses, creating incredible sensations.

She hadn't known she could absorb this much stimulation without release. But Kane had carefully stoked the heat, the increments so tiny that her body kept adjusting, then requiring more. She pulled on the bindings. Her ragged breath barely filled her starving lungs.

And Kane and the Hard Copies kept upping the friction. Her breasts swelled and each flick of tongue on her nipples shot fire straight to her core, where Kane matched fire with more fire, building a conflagration. Kane was pushing her beyond her limits.

If she hadn't been bound, she would have been

clawing at him to enter her. She would have been twisting and turning to capture his sex between her thighs. And as more droplets trickled over her flesh, she was going out of her mind with need.

"I can't take…much more."

Silence answered her.

And yet even as she bit back a few choice swear words, her body leaped to a new place—a plane where every puff of air, every twist and clenching of her muscles rippled pleasure over her skin. Not enough for release, but her own movement caused further arousal. Her own breathing caused her nipples to tighten. Just thinking about the heat between her thighs fed the fire.

He'd caused this marvelous sensation. And now it was time for him to finish.

"Kane?" His name on her lips came out more whimper than demand.

"Yes?"

"I need you."

"Okay."

She felt tugging at her wrists and her hands were freed. Other hands on her ankles freed her feet.

She shoved the blindfold from her eyes. Kane knelt on the bed, frowning as the Hard Copies disappeared, melting into their components and flowing like a river back into the red case.

"It's your fault."

"What?" She tackled him and he rolled onto his back. Without hesitation she straddled him and took him inside her.

He lifted his hips to meet her halfway. His hands closed over her breasts. "Maintaining the Hard Copies...takes concentration."

"So?" She rode him, leaning forward, allowing his sex to rub her sweet spot. Nothing had ever felt so delightful.

"So...all I could think about was...you."

A roar filled her ears. Her muscles clenched around his hardness and she spasmed so violently that streaks of bold red and slashes of oranges seared through her. Talk about seeing stars. She saw an entire galaxy.

And beneath her Kane took control, holding her hips, thrusting into her with powerful lunges. Somehow he maintained the exact angle she liked most and kept the pressure on her pulsing core, until one explosion expanded into a series that took away her breath and blew away her thoughts.

Unbelievable pleasure caught her in a vortex, shooting her higher, bursting, then rocketing her higher again. Her fingers and toes went numb. Her body turned electric, sensation zinging from head to foot and back again, feeding on itself, escalating, extracting every iota of energy from her in order to fuel the explosions.

She writhed wildly. Her body shattered. And she lost all sense of time and place. She no longer knew where she began and Kane ended. It was as though they'd merged into one.

13

THEIR NIGHT TOGETHER might have started with incredible orgasms but it ended on a tender note. Fallon had no idea how long it took her to recover from those first series of orgasms, but afterwards she dozed and woke up sometime in the middle of the night wrapped in Kane's strong arms.

Sensing that he was awake, she snuggled into his warmth. His proximity reminded her that the time bubble was collapsing. However, if that kept them close during their remaining time, she certainly wouldn't object. She loved waking up with his scent on her skin, his heartbeat in her ear as she cuddled against his chest. "You are amazing."

"*We* are amazing." He smoothed her hair back from her face. "If there was any way at all that I could stay with you, I would do so."

"I know." She didn't want to think about him leaving. "If there was a way for me to go to the future, I would do it."

Surprise lightened his tone. "You'd leave your family? Your business?"

"Yes." She didn't hesitate. This time had shown

her that her family had to learn to manage without her. She'd always believed they'd needed her, but perhaps she'd had to believe that to make up for what lacked in her personal life.

Even after Kane left, she was determined not to repeat her mistakes. She needn't be so ready to solve her family's problems. She needn't be so available. She needed to let them stand on their own. And she had plenty of work to keep her busy. While so much of the recent cancer work looked promising, there was more money to raise, more scientists to whom she wished to offer grants. Work had always satisfied her, but now she wanted more.

If only Kane could stay. Or she could go. But wishing that they had a lifetime couldn't alter the laws of physics. The time bubble was shrinking.

"I have no regrets." She spoke past the lump in her throat. "I would rather have loved you than never loved at all."

He groaned and rolled on top of her, supporting his weight on his elbows, his hands cupping her face. "I want you to live a full, happy life. Will you do that for me?"

"Yes." Heart breaking, she wound her arms around his neck. "I shall miss you terribly. But you have given me something precious."

"Wonderful orgasms?" he teased.

"That too." She tugged his mouth close. "But you've taught me that I can't ignore the part of me that loves. Even if I find another—"

"And I hope you will."

"It will be because you taught me how to trust that part of myself."

She spoke softly but her inner thoughts churned with turmoil. She didn't want to find another man. She wanted Kane. She wanted to spend the rest of her life with him. She wanted to bear his children. She wanted them to grow old together. Damn it. Of all the men in the world to love, why did she have to want the one who had no choice but to leave her?

She had too much self-control to let him know how much she was hurting. For his sake, she would get a firm grip and hold it together. After he left would be the time to grieve and heal.

And she could no longer hide the truth from herself. Losing him would be the same as death. And, in fact, she'd be dead decades before he would be born. Her stomach rocked and pitched. Despite her effort to hide her churning thoughts from Kane, her body was protesting. Recognizing she was going to be sick, she dashed to the bathroom and slammed the door.

Kane opened it to find her heaving. Another man would have closed the door and left her alone to her misery. Kane calmly ran water over a washcloth, wrung it out and handed it to her. "I'm sorry. You may be suffering from residual effects of the shrinking time bubble."

She spat in the toilet and wiped her mouth. Shaky, she used a toothbrush by the sink and rinsed with mouthwash. To his credit, he didn't pester her with questions and she used the time to pull her thoughts in order. If he thought her sickness was due to the time bubble and not the thought of losing him, she had no intention of enlightening him.

He might not be able to give her even another twenty-four hours, but she could give him the peace of mind that she would be fine going on without him. Drawing on an inner strength she'd used whenever life didn't go her way, she took his hand and led him back to bed, determined not to let her nausea get in the way of what might very well be their last night together.

They snuggled for a while and her stomach settled. They made love again. Slowly. Gently. Tenderly. This time there was no further use of the Hot Copier. There was simply one man, one woman. And she cherished every moment, adored the way he could change from domineering to playful to tender. Loving this man was always an adventure, never routine. And she would miss him with every cell in her body. But despite wanting to capture every precious moment in her memory, her body had its own demands. She could stay awake for only so long.

And when they awakened in the early hours of the morning, she would have liked to have made love once more, but Kane was all business. "Sorry. But I have to find Nigel, today."

"How?" she asked, padding naked to the shower and wishing she'd brought a fresh set of clothes to change into. Although this was Vegas and the casinos were open 24/7, the shops didn't have those same hours. Not even the concierge could send up new clothes this early.

"He's running out of time. Can you arrange for someone else to take care of buying this technology?"

"Sure. I'll make certain it's a high enough bid that I can't lose." She stepped under the water and let it sluice over her. One of the advantages of running an empire was she had bankers who were more than willing to help and lawyers on the payroll to oversee the transaction.

"Nigel has to convert the funds to hard assets and then store them someplace that won't be disturbed for over a century. With the help of the Shey Group we can follow the money trail."

"What will they do to help?" she asked as he joined her in the shower. She wanted to distract him with her hands and her mouth, but he soaped, rinsed and shampooed, all business, and she understood that time was of the essence.

"Logan Kincaid assured me that he can follow the funds. He has computer specialists who can tap into your systems. And once he informs me where the money is and where it's going, we should be able to intercept Nigel."

"And how will you stop him when he has strength-enhancing implants and you don't?"

Kane chuckled. "I have a…machine…that will ice him."

"You're going to kill him?"

He shook his head. "I'll literally freeze him at a cellular level."

She frowned. "Cells are made of water. When

water freezes, it expands and ruptures the cells. You're going to kill him."

He shook his head. "Science has come a long way since…now. I don't understand the process myself. All I know is that I point the gun, pull the trigger and a direct hit prepares his body to go forward to his own time."

"But he's going forward anyway. Why do you have to send him?"

"Because my device will put him in a detention center. If he goes back on his own, finding him will be almost impossible. We have many privacy laws to protect us. Unfortunately, they also protect the guilty. Hiding in my time is actually much easier than here."

Fallon got the idea that there was much Kane wasn't telling her. For all she knew, once Nigel returned he could change his DNA along with his appearance. She supposed it didn't matter. All she really needed to understand was that today might be Kane's last chance to complete his mission successfully.

Although he'd remained closemouthed about so much of the future, she understood that Nigel was a serious threat. But even if she hadn't, she would have helped Kane—because she loved him.

FALLON DROVE the rental car, following Kane's directions. The desert sun heated the car and she turned up the AC. Kane hadn't told her that the closer they got to his departure time, the faster the bubble would collapse. She had to stay within ten feet of him or the nausea would kick in.

In the car, maintaining the close proximity was obviously easy. But she feared that once they confronted Nigel, she might slow Kane down. They'd returned to their hotel room earlier for a weapon and he'd donned the suit he'd worn when he'd arrived. While he hadn't specifically said he needed to wear the special material to time travel, he also didn't speak about the weapon he shoved into a holster at his hip, which then disappeared. If she hadn't already bought vanishing technology she might have doubted her eyes or her sanity.

Fallon's cell phone rang and she hit the speaker button so Kane could hear. "Hello."

"Ms. Hanover," her banker spoke crisply, "we transferred the funds as you requested."

"Thank you."

"It's our pleasure doing business with you. If there's anything else, please don't hesitate to let us know."

She ended the call. "Done."

"You understand that it's essential that the Hot Copier and all the documentation is destroyed, don't you? Logan Kincaid will help you do this."

"I understand."

At that moment, another call came in. "Hello."

"Logan Kincaid, here."

Speak of the devil. "Logan, I have you on speakerphone. Kane is next to me."

"The funds that you wired to a Las Vegas bank were immediately transferred to a bank in the Cayman Islands, then Switzerland, Bulgaria, Singapore and then back to Las Vegas. From there, Nigel made significant purchases all over town. Ten million in precious gemstones, twenty million in art, ten million in security bonds backed by the U.S. government and another ten in miscellaneous quit claim deeds."

"Can you pinpoint Nigel's location?" Kane asked.

"He's hired armored trucks to pick up the loot. The drivers don't know their destinations. However, we have located and are tracking every truck by GPS. Satellite imaging analysis projects with eighty-five percent certainty that the trucks will converge in one hour at the Hoover Dam."

"You'll continue to track and notify us if there's any changes?"

"Of course. Would you like backup?"

"Thank you but that won't be necessary."

Kane hung up the phone and must have read her thoughts. *She* would have liked backup. "The fewer people around Nigel, the less likely he'll change the future. I can't take a chance of him injuring or killing anyone."

She knew that included her. All along Kane had been worried that keeping her with him would place her in danger. She patted her purse and the gun inside that the Shey Group had provided. Thanks to her CIA training, she could handle herself.

"So what's the plan?" she asked.

"We find Nigel. I ice him and send him back where he belongs."

"And then you leave?" She glanced at him and his total stoicism told her he was fighting his feelings as much as she was.

"Then I leave." He turned to her then. "I wish I could say I was sorry for getting you into this mess, but I'm not."

She didn't know whether to laugh or cry at his admission. And she wished she could say something sassy or saucy to lighten the moment, but she didn't dare speak for fear her voice would crack. Instead, at a red light, she reached over and squeezed his hand, letting go after it turned green.

Kane didn't speak for several minutes and when he did, he changed the subject. "Nigel will be there to unload the trucks. Hopefully he'll be distracted and I can take him out before he sees us. But if not, I may have to move fast. Try and stay with me and I'll do my best to protect you."

"Got it."

Kane's tone hardened. "I intend to keep him too busy to notice you. So don't do anything to draw his attention."

"Understood." She spoke firmly but hadn't agreed to anything. She thought he hadn't noticed but he frowned at her and she pointed to the road. "Do we turn here?"

He checked the map. "Keep going straight."

When Hoover Dam came into view, the amazing sight of thousands of tons of concrete holding back all that water wasn't what drew her eyes. She'd been here before as a tourist. It was the giant traffic jam that made her wonder if they'd arrived too late. Four armored trucks blocked part of the highway. Instead of police officers ticketing the trucks, they seemed to be directing traffic to wait. With the road a virtual parking lot, they were at a complete stop and going nowhere.

"Pull onto the shoulder," Kane directed. "Let's hope he's not monitoring and doesn't pick up the signal from my high-tech equipment."

Fallon thought that unlikely. Nigel knew Kane was on his trail. He had to be aware he was vulnerable while he saw to all the treasures he'd bought.

After exiting the car, they sprinted past the stopped traffic, keeping the vehicles between them and the other side of the highway where a man was signaling for the trucks to use an off-ramp onto a side road.

"He's likely found an old tunnel into the dam or the mountain where he intends to store his loot." Kane spoke easily as he ran, not the least bit out of breath.

Fallon wished she could say the same. She needed to make time to work out more. No way was she in the same kind of shape as Kane. Still, she didn't think she'd be this badly off from running a quarter of a mile. Although she'd already broken into a light sweat and her breath was labored, it was the simultaneous feeling of hot and flushed on the outside and cold and trembling inside that warned her she couldn't keep up the pace much longer. However, Kane had told her one of the key elements to his plan was surprise. She didn't want to slow him down and give Nigel a chance to see them on his monitor.

Kane found a spot where they could leave the highway, hopefully unobserved. He cut swiftly into the shadows of the steep bank alongside, his steps as quiet and lethal as a mountain cat's in search of prey.

He must have sensed her lagging because he stopped, although he kept his gaze following the trucks that rumbled into the mountain. They traveled along what looked like an old railroad spur that hadn't been used in decades. She speculated that the original contractors might have used the spur to carry materials over the tracks during the initial building of the dam. It was one of many government projects designed to employ workers and help the country out of the Great Depression. Likely, the tunnel had stood for almost a century and would last undisturbed for another—an excellent hiding place.

"I don't like this," Kane muttered.

"What?"

"The first truck is coming out."

"You think he'll report seeing us to Nigel?" She didn't understand Kane's concern as they headed inside.

"There appears to be only this one way in."

"That means Nigel can't get past us." She removed her gun from her purse and tucked it into her jacket pocket. If necessary, she could shoot right through the material without drawing the weapon. Although she understood that Kane intended to take Nigel back alive, she liked to keep her options open.

"It also could be a trap."

"You think he went to all this trouble to get you off his trail?"

"Nigel is very intelligent. He's schemed well. It's never wise to underestimate one's opponent."

The tunnel smelled of old dust and dirt. Without the sun to warm her, the temperature dropped ten degrees. And as the sweat from her run dried on her flesh, she felt icy all over. Putting down her condition to fear, determined not to hinder Kane in any way—physically or mentally—she shoved her discomfort to the back of her mind.

The truck fumes were thick and the air made her a little sick. She didn't understand why the trucks weren't turning off their engines to unload. The smell didn't seem to bother Kane, so she put down her sensitivity to nerves.

Headlights lit a scene of a crew of men unloading crates onto handheld dollies and rolling them through a doorway beyond their vision. The trucks' engines covered any noisy steps they might have made.

"Do you see Nigel?" she asked softly.

"No. How do you feel about hijacking the last truck?" Kane asked.

"Hijacking it?"

He didn't explain. Kane's suit magically changed and now matched the men's uniforms. "Follow me."

Kane trotted to the last truck and knocked on the door. The driver opened the truck and Kane jerked his thumb over his shoulder, speaking to both security guards while she kept out of sight. "They need more help up at the—"

A bright light flared out of Kane's wrist, a light he carefully kept aimed below the dash so none of the other guards would spot it. The flash of light had come from a tiny tubular device he held that he quickly slid up his sleeve. The light had caused both men to slump unconscious and Kane opened the door, dragged one man to the ground and then went back for his partner.

She climbed into the passenger seat and he tossed a shirt and cap her way, then slid behind the wheel. "You okay?"

"I'm fine. What about those guys?"

"They'll wake up in a few hours with nothing more than a few aching muscles."

She removed her jacket, shrugged into the shirt, shoved her hair under the cap and pulled it low over her eyes. Then she transferred her gun into the waistband of her slacks. Not as good an option as her jacket, but the weapon made her feel more in control.

Kane stepped on the gas and they jerked forward. Then he jammed on the brake, almost throwing her into the dash. "Sorry, the pedals are touchier than I thought."

"You do know how to drive, don't you?" she asked.

"Last time I drove a petroleum-propelled vehicle it was before World War One."

"If that was supposed to make me feel better, it didn't."

"Don't worry. I'll get the hang of it soon."

He eased forward more smoothly this time and she let out a sigh of relief. "You don't have trucks in the future, either?"

"You already know entirely too much about the future." He stepped on the brake a little too hard again but at least this time she didn't fear she'd go through the windshield.

The truck in front of them unloaded slowly, giving them time to look over the site. But there wasn't much to see. Four men unloaded the truck, working in teams. Two hefted the heavy crates down to the other team who loaded the dollies and disappeared for a minute before returning empty.

"They are returning for the next load so quickly, they can't be going far." He angled the truck's side mirror. "I'd like an advance peek into that area before we go in. I'm hoping it's small enough that you can stay outside and still remain in the time bubble."

The driver got back into the truck in front of them and then did a five-point turnaround and headed out the tunnel. Kane pulled up smoothly, yanked on the brake and opened the door, but not before glancing into the sideview mirror.

She caught sight of a small room, filled floor to ceiling with boxes and lit by the truck's headlights. No one appeared to be inside, but perhaps the angle was wrong.

By the time she'd exited and rounded the front of the vehicle, he'd KO'd the two men who'd been manning the dollies. He dragged both to one side while she unlocked the back of the vehicle.

The truck was stuffed with crates, all marked by lettering that read Hazardous Material. She shoved two smallish crates onto the ground. On the other side of each crate was a radiation symbol—no doubt to hide the precious items from thieves that might return if they knew the real contents. Kane joined her and loaded the dolly so high that he'd be hidden from view to anyone in the room when he pushed it inside.

Staying behind him, she slipped to one side of the doorway as he rolled the dolly on through. Wishing she could see, heart pounding, she tensed, drew her gun from her waistband and listened hard.

She heard an impatient and distracted voice mutter, "Took you long enough. Set the load in that corner. And be careful. If these crates break open, the contents will poison us."

Kane grunted. At her angle from outside, she could see him swing the dolly to one side and reach for the icing device at his hip with his free hand. The next moment, Nigel knocked Kane down with such force that he shot backward, stirring up a cloud of dust.

As badly as she wanted to help Kane by shooting Nigel, she didn't dare, not with the dust making it difficult for her to see. With the two men rolling and jabbing elbows and knees, if she shot the gun she was as likely to hit Kane as Nigel.

The smaller man fought like a dynamo and with a strength that more than equaled Kane's, despite his larger frame. Vicious grunts, the smacking of flesh on flesh, kicks and punches made the dust thicken. As much as she feared entering the room might distract Kane, she wanted to help, and she edged closer, waiting for an opportunity.

When the men crashed into a wall near her, she slammed her gun into Nigel's temple. He cursed in pain, shifted and kicked the gun from her hand, but his fingers remained clenched firmly around Kane's throat.

Her gun skittered across the floor. She advanced warily. Voice hoarse, Kane roared at her. "Get out."

She ignored him. Until Nigel's enhancers wore off, Kane was at a distinct disadvantage. And if Kane lost, Nigel would kill her anyway—she knew too much about his treasure.

Leaving wasn't an option. If only she could find her gun. But between the fighting bodies, the crates and the dust, she could barely see.

The men smashed into a pile of crates beside her and one of them split open. A golden artifact with ruby eyes glinted in the truck's headlights. She hefted it, testing its weight. A perfect weapon.

Fallon crouched, holding the sculpture, waiting for an opportunity. In the small space, the men's fighting hadn't slowed. Kane slammed a knee into Nigel's chest. His air went out with a soft *oof*, but he rolled away and like a gymnast regained his feet.

Kane's breath was labored and she feared his lungs had been starved of oxygen too long from the strangling to keep him going. Yet, he, too, dragged himself to his feet. The men circled, looking for an opening.

Nigel lunged.

Kane shifted, tried to sweep his opponent off his feet. But the enhancers rooted Nigel and Kane was the one who fell. He went down hard and rolled. But Nigel dived on top of him, striking with a series of blows to the body and face.

Fallon waited, wincing at each smack of knuckles on flesh. Waited until Nigel's back was to her. And then she pounced.

14

OUT OF HIS swelling eye, Kane caught sight of a golden object whizzing by, then thunking Nigel's thick skull. Fallon's effort dazed Nigel, giving Kane the moment he required to retrieve the icer, shove it against Nigel's side and pull the trigger.

"Bastard!" Nigel swore and then toppled over, instantly incapacitated.

Fallon dropped the golden statue and flung her arms around Kane's neck. "Are you all right?"

Ignoring his bruised chest, aching bones and battered face, he drew her into his arms in a fierce embrace. "Thank you. I didn't want you to place yourself at risk, but thank you."

She trembled in his arms and he could feel her tears on his neck. "I thought he was going to kill you."

Her concern had been all about him. He doubted she'd once considered her own safety and his heart ached for this woman. Now that Nigel was on ice, the bubble was shrinking rapidly. "We have only a few minutes."

"I don't want you to go."

"I don't want to go." He tightened his arms, appreciating the way her curves molded to him. Even covered in dust, she smelled good. And as he thought how she'd risked her life to help him, he knew that she was his heart. No one would ever take her place.

A lump rose in his throat as he acknowledged his love. But he bit back the words. He wanted her to look to her future, not the past. He couldn't stay. He'd known from the beginning this moment would arrive. He'd tried to deny his feelings—and failed miserably.

Fallon was part of him. Losing her would be like losing the best part of himself. Anguish and frustration battled with a need to use these last moments wisely. He tamped down his grief over losing her, forcing himself to think past the crushing loss to focus on the present.

"I'm leaving soon. And this treasure cache is yours. Your money paid for it. Keep these things or sell them."

She stiffened and lifted her mouth to his, gently kissing his swollen and split lip. "I don't care about the money."

"I know." He rocked her against him. "As the bubble collapses, you'll feel sick."

"I'm already sick at the thought of you leaving me," she admitted, then spoke more strongly, likely pulling herself together for his sake. "But I won't regret our time together. Not ever."

He tried to keep her in the middle of the collapsing bubble to protect her from the worst of the ill effects. "We had something special together. Now we will both go on."

"Yes."

He said the words to bolster her courage, knowing he would never find another woman he loved as much as Fallon. But now was not the time for truth. Beside them Nigel disappeared.

"He's gone." Fallon clutched him so tightly, as if the time bubble wouldn't separate them. But physics didn't work that way. His trip back was one way. He'd never see her again.

He had mere seconds left. "Goodbye, my darling Fallon."

FALLON NEVER KNEW how long she'd sat in the dust after Kane popped out of her existence. The time bubble's effects seemed to have taken a long time to dissipate. Her stomach had still churned but eventually she'd shoved to her feet, just in time to meet Logan Kincaid and his Shey Group. He'd assured her his people would see that the treasure was safely shipped to her home. And no doubt recognizing her state of shock and inability to think clearly, he'd insisted that a doctor look her over to make sure she hadn't been injured.

The doctor had done a complete physical. She hadn't had the strength to object. And now she sat in his office, waiting to leave Las Vegas, her thoughts numb. She had hundreds of calls to return, business decisions to make, a family to reassure. But all she could think about was how she was going to go on with her life without Kane.

"Still feeling shaky, Ms. Hanover?"

She nodded, not trusting herself to speak.

"After a life-threatening experience, it's normal to be on edge. And in your condition, it's even likelier."

"My condition?"

"I believe you're pregnant. It's a bit too early to confirm but—"

"What?"

"The vomiting. The cold chills and hot flashes. Your sensitivity to smells."

Her symptoms were classic. But she'd blamed the time bubble and her upset. For a smart woman she hadn't been thinking clearly since Kane had popped into her world.

They hadn't used birth control. She'd been so aroused from his creativity, the idea hadn't crossed her mind.

Oh…my…God. She was pregnant. With Kane's baby.

Her hand curled protectively over her womb. She might not have Kane, but she had a precious piece of him.

A baby. The idea floated and wrapped around her like warm and fuzzy fleece.

She wondered if Kane would ever know. Would he look her up in history, see the date of the baby's birth and realize they'd made a child? A child who would die before his father was born. The idea made her head ache and her heart shatter.

"Ms. Hanover, are you all right?" the doctor asked.

From the sound of the doc's voice, he'd asked the question a few times and she hadn't heard. Rousing herself from the chair and her thoughts, she gathered her purse, thanked him and left the office.

She had plans to make. And one thing she knew for certain. She didn't want to work full-time and raise her child, too. Fallon had all the respect in the world for working mothers, but she wanted to see her child's first smile, hear his or her first word, and she would miss so much if she went back to her former life.

Fallon's mind whirled with plans. She would find good managers and put them in charge of each corporation, promoting from inside where she could. She'd redecorate her home and make it child friendly.

Kane probably hadn't realized he'd given her a precious gift, a reason to live. And she would do something for him in return. Determined to put her plan in motion, she picked up her phone and called her attorney. And while she was arranging a gift for the father, she would make out a new will. She would soon have an heir, and as the sole parent she would prepare for all contingencies.

KANE'S FIRST FEW DAYS back were filled with making certain Nigel was incarcerated and placed into rehab and with his own thorough debriefing. The Time Line Guardians had to go over his every move to ensure he had not compromised the time continuum.

His superiors were not happy that Fallon had been

caught in the time bubble and knew so much about the future. But for some reason beyond his understanding, they weren't as upset as he'd feared. The day they released him from containment, he went straight to the chronology library and found out the reason his boss had let him off with no more than a ten-point penalty in his work file.

Two months after Kane had left Fallon, she'd died in a plane crash.

The news hit hard. He'd always known Fallon would be long dead when he'd arrived back in his time. But to learn her life had been cut so short made him angry with grief. It was like losing her all over again. Pain washed through him. No wonder his bosses hadn't been concerned. Fallon hadn't lived long enough to do anything with the knowledge he'd given her.

Saddened, Kane slumped in the library, wishing he could have done something, anything, to save her. If only he'd known her history, he could have warned her not to fly. If he'd known, he would have broken every rule to tell her how to avoid her untimely death. He might have risked changing history and all their futures to save her—he loved her that much.

Now there was nothing he could do to save her. The laws of physics would not permit him to go back. No one could travel to the same time twice. He had no way to warn her. No way to help her. No way to save her. Or was there?

He racked his brains, staring hard at the picture of the plane's explosion. And then he reread the story, his excitement escalating and his heart racing. His idea was wild. Crazy. But was it meant to be?

FALLON STRAPPED her seat belt across her lap, but not too tightly. She didn't want to constrict her baby in the womb. She supposed the thought of protecting it was silly. At two months her child couldn't be even an inch long.

Having cut almost all her business ties, Fallon was satisfied with the new direction her life had taken. She'd liquidated her assets, simplified her life and was gratified to learn that the people she'd hand-picked to run her charity foundations and the Hanover empire were doing a good job.

She was even more pleased that her family was getting along without her constant supervision. Although her parents and sister had all objected to her raising her "love child" alone, she paid them no heed, seeing their objections for what they really were: fear that she'd have less time to cater to them.

Kane had taught Fallon that her family could only take advantage of her if she let them. And she no longer would let them. She only accepted one call every few days from her relatives and had found that not only was her life more peaceful, but that they could manage without her.

As she sipped an orange juice before takeoff, she decided this would be her last ride in the private jet for a while. Traveling seemed to upset her system now that she was pregnant. So she was heading back to Tampa to stay there until she gave birth.

Fallon closed her eyes during the takeoff, appreciating the swift lift into the air. She ignored her stomach and took a few crackers from her purse. Eating frequently and at the first sign of stomach upset often kept the nausea under control. What she didn't understand was why they called it morning sickness when she was sick all damn day. It was really a wonder that some women went through more than one pregnancy. She didn't feel beautiful. She didn't glow. She felt ill and the turbulence wasn't helping.

She pressed a toggle that allowed her to speak directly to the pilot. "Captain Evans?"

"Sorry about the turbulence, ma'am. We should be above it once we clear five thousand feet."

"Thank you."

Fallon recalled the instantaneous travel she'd experienced with Kane and wished she could snap her fingers and instantly be home. But that wasn't all she remembered and all she longed for. She missed Kane, more than she'd thought possible.

Although the baby gave her something to look forward to, she wished they could raise him together. Kane might never know he had a child. He certainly wouldn't meet him. He wouldn't be there to teach him how to be strong and tender. He wouldn't be there to give him what he deserved: the wonderful father she knew Kane would be.

Her eyes teared. And she angrily wiped away the wetness, annoyed with her weakness.

Kane had given her more than she'd ever expected, but she couldn't deny she missed talking to him, holding him, making love. To know that she would never see him again was awful, but to know that their child would never meet his father was tragic.

The plane leaped like a bucking bronco and her drink sailed into the aisle. A popping noise alarmed her and then the oxygen mask dropped from the ceiling. In all the years she'd been flying, this had never happened. Her pulse sped but she told herself to be calm. Stress wasn't good for the baby.

But neither was a crashing airplane.

Oh…God.

The nose dived. Through the window, an engine burst into flames.

Captain Evan's voice remained calm. "The right engine has failure. We're going down. Brace for impact."

Could they fly under one engine? She didn't dare ask the captain, certain he had other things to do. Like setting them down in a field. A nice open field with no trees. No electric wires. But visualizing them setting down lightly was almost impossible. Smoke poured through the cabin. The deck under her feet pitched from side to side.

They were falling. Falling out of control.

Her fingers gripped the armrests in a desperate attempt to prevent herself from being thrown from side to side. Adrenaline pumped through her, but there was nowhere to run. Nowhere to hide.

And as the plane plummeted, she realized that if the pilot didn't pull up the nose, there was no hope.

She and the baby were going to die.

Looking out the window at the topsy-turvy landscape caused panic to rip through her. The treetops scraped the underbelly. The plane pitched to the right.

The G-force made holding up her head difficult. And then flames shot through the cabin. Heat blasted. Fire poured through the cabin, blackening, incinerating.

Fallon closed her eyes and prepared to die.

15

KANE KINCAID couldn't let her die. Even if they sent him to rehab, saving Fallon would be worth whatever it cost him.

And so he strode into the time laboratory, a building that perched next to the Caribbean Sea, as if he had every right to be there. As if the move wasn't risky.

He prayed the experiment would work. If he failed, she would die at his hands. But if he didn't act, she was going to die anyway. He triple-checked his calculations, then adjusted the calibrations on his machine by a smidgeon. Plucking her out of time at the exact moment before her death was tricky, but it was pinpointing her exact location as the plane plunged, and the earth spun on it axis and through its orbit that were critical.

Kane's fingers flew into the holographic imaging, adjusting infinitesimal nanopoints to ensure the time bubble formed around all of her and didn't accidentally lop off a limb. Sweat beaded his forehead as the computer counted down.

"Three."

"Two."

"One."

"Commence time transfer."

For a permanent transfer, Kane always expected the time bubble simply to transport an object through the folds of space instantaneously—but it didn't work that way. For every action there had to be an equal and opposite reaction and so as he pulled Fallon forward he sent the exact same amount of mass backward, metal that would fuse with the airplane as it plunged, and by the time it struck the ground, it would appear no different from the rest of the crashed airplane.

He didn't want Fallon simply to visit his time, he wanted her to stay. And when the time forces shunted her through the portal, without a suit to protect her, he prayed she'd be whole, uninjured, alive.

He had no right to take her from everyone and everything she'd ever known—but surely she'd prefer life to death. He paced from one side of the laboratory to another, ignoring the beautiful sunset beyond the portal. He clenched and unclenched his fingers a hundred times.

And then she was there, stepping through the portal, a gorgeous sight for his worried eyes. She didn't look healthy though. As he reached to steady her, she shuddered and swallowed hard, the green tinge of her skin making him wonder if he'd made her ill.

"Kane? Am I dead?" Confusion clouded her beautiful eyes.

"Your plane was about to crash, so I brought you to the future."

She blinked, as if she didn't believe her eyes. "The future?"

He stashed his disappointment that she hadn't immediately thrown herself into his arms. He had to remind himself that she must have been terrified in that plunging plane, and then the time bubble might have seemed like moving on toward death.

Gently, he led her to a chair and handed her a glass of water. "Take it easy and I'll explain." She sipped, then craned her neck to look up at him. Kneeling he took her hand. "You were about to die in the plane crash. So I brought you forward."

"I'm in the future?" She shook her head. "You said that was impossible."

"I said it had never been done—"

"Because it would change history." She frowned at him. "What have you done?"

"No one's ever been pulled forward for fear of changing history. But how could I be changing the past when I pulled you out of time right before your plane crashed?"

"Maybe I would have survived."

He shook his head. "Although the pilot and one female crew member lived, your body was never found."

"What?"

"Don't you see? For all we know, we aren't changing history. I did exactly what I was meant to do—pull you out of your time and into mine."

"You had permission to save me?" She looked around the lab, as if searching for his superiors and when she spied no one, her puzzled gaze returned to his.

"I don't give a damn what my superiors think. You are worth more to me than my career."

"They'll fire you?"

He shrugged. "I wanted you to live."

"Will your bosses forgive you when you send me back?"

She might look ill but she was thinking clearly. He squeezed her hand. "You aren't going back."

"But when the time bubble—"

"I sent back an equal mass of metal to take your place. You're here for good. No way could I let you die."

She didn't say anything for a moment and his heart stopped. Then she broke into a brilliant smile, leaned over and kissed him. God. She tasted like a fresh summer shower.

Her arms closed around him. "I missed you so much."

"So you don't mind marrying a man who's about to be unemployed?"

Her eyes darkened. "You love your work and now you'll lose your job. I'm so sorry."

"It was worth it. I love you. But you're accustomed to wealth and—"

"Shh. I love you." She leaned her head against his shoulder. "And I'm so glad we can be together." Relief filled him and then her lips turned up mischievously. "I have a surprise for you."

She hadn't known she was coming forward. How could she possibly have a surprise for him?

"We're having a baby." Tears of joys brimmed in her eyes. "I'm pregnant."

Adrenaline washed through him. He had the woman he loved and she was pregnant with their child. He couldn't have been more pleased. He now had every thing he wanted. Fallon. A baby. "You've made me a happy man."

She grinned. "Wait until you see what you're getting for your birthday."

Her statement pleased him, but alarmed him. Fallon had been a wealthy woman. She was going to have to learn to make do on what he could earn. "Now, we don't have a lot of money. And no elaborate gifts are required. You and the baby are all the presents I need."

She laughed at him. "Remember Nigel's stash?"

"Yeah?"

"Well, I hid it along with some other things in my basement vault. The Shey Group has kept the place safe for all these years."

"For me?"

"I deeded it to you for your thirtieth birthday."

He kissed her again. "Did I ever tell you how amazing you are?"

"No. And you never told me you loved me until now, either. But I already knew." Her tone rang with satisfaction as she urged him to his feet. "I can't wait to see this world, but there's something I want more."

"What?" He would have given her anything, this precious, marvelous woman who made him feel whole.

"Take me someplace private. Very private."

He laughed and threw his arm over his shoulder. "That, I can do."